"PUNCHINELLO
and other bandroom brawls . . ."

J. C. WADSWORTH

Thanks for cover illustrations to JOFF KENYON

ISBN 1904908365

Printed by
Kirklees Music

609 Bradford Road, Bailiff Bridge, Brighouse, West Yorkshire HD6 4DN
Tel: (01484) 722855 - Fax: (01484) 723591 – E-mail: sales@kirkleesmusic.co.uk
www.kirkleesmusic.co.uk

ABOUT THE AUTHOR

Janet Wadsworth, writer of novels and short stories, former canal boat builder and teacher, living in the musical heart of West Yorkshire, the Holme Valley, respects and enjoys the brass band world partly because she's married to Kevin, member of Black Dyke Mills Band for sixteen glorious years who has since played in and conducted more than a score of other bands.

"Punchinello ..." is a collection of stories reflecting the life, the music and the personalities involved in being a member, or supporter, of a brass band. Each chapter is a musical piece, the whole a complete performance.

FOREWORD

Punchinello is a fictitious tale about a very real group of people who make up the brass band movement and who – by and large – are the salt of the earth. I am sure that, like me, hundreds of "band-chaps" will be able to trace their careers through the story and recognise many of the story's heroes along the way.

It's all here, the elation of winning, the pathos of a bandsman's funeral, strong friendships that last throughout life, and above all the humour and the joy of making music through the magic that's a brass band.

My own journey through the band world began in 1943, but it was when I came under the tutelage of Mr J W Morley, after his return from the war in 1945, that I realised that "banding" was for me. I won more than a hundred slow melody prizes over the years. I served with the RAF Regiment Band doubling tuba and bass trombone from 1949 – 51. 1962 saw me move up into the heights with the Carlton Main Frickley Colliery Band as bass trombone and secretary for 23 years. On the collapse of the mining industry I returned to Skelmanthorpe as MD, in later years taking responsibility for the development of young players.

Through my career I've been lucky enough to be player, administrator, conductor, and adjudicator but I've found the greatest privilege to be in developing the talents of the young.

Laurence Mann M.B.E.

PROGRAMME

Dedicated to all bands

New Beginnings

'D'you ever think about what you might have done if you hadn't plumbed?'

It was warm for early April, a late Saturday afternoon, and Horny and Stirling were sitting on the low wall outside the pub, supping their third pints and thoughtfully watching the local girls undressed for their big night out. It therefore took some time for the question to seep through the several layers of fluffy lagging wrapping Stirling's mind.

Horny asked again.

'If you hadn't been a plumber what might you have done?'

Stirling took a long, thoughtful drink. Then another.

'That's a 'ard one,' he said finally. 'It's easy for you. You've bloody tried most things. Me, I've always really liked fitting pieces of pipe together wi' elbow joints. It's like a game, you know.' He settled his back against his own bit of the pub wall. 'When we was kids do you remember 'ow we used to spend hours damming the stream up above Holme? It's not quite the same, but at least now I get bloody paid for it.'

They watched another group of girls squawking their way towards the bus stop.

'Easy to see why they call 'em hen nights,' said Stirling, fascinated. 'How do their ear drums stand it?'

'Aren't you glad you're not young?' Horny asked. 'Well, in one way. Certainly it looks cold to be young nowadays.'

'Never thought I'd hear you bloody complaining about the amount of clothes some lasses aren't wearing,' said Stirling.

'So?' asked Horny.

'What? If I hadn't gone in for plumbing? I mind when a recruiting sergeant came to school and I thought about joining the foreign legion or whatever it were. I were in a bloody great hole with old Hopalong Hepple and maths homework.' He laughed. 'Then Palmer enlisted and that were it for me. Edwin Palmer. Remember him? Never got picked for football.'

The next bus load of girls paraded past.

'They're the winners,' breathed Horny, awe in his voice. 'Just look at that tall girl with the very short … Mind you, you can see from here that she's cold.'

'But d'you know what? I'm sure it were 'im on tele t'other night. I said to our Dolores, 'In't that that twerp Edwin Palmer? But 'e's got a bloody moustache? 'Ow's 'e managed to grow that? Never thought he'd manage it." He drained his glass, held it up and looked expectantly at Horny. 'Anyroad, he were a general in Iraq. It just shows.'

'Shows what? And it's your round.'

Stirling grumbled his way to the bar and struggled back, glasses held high above the heads of the crowd. He put the two full glasses down on the wall between them and licked the froth from his fingers.

'So what brought all this thinking on? And why are you looking so bloody happy? You've got no right. We're going to be bloody late as usual for Bernard's special rehearsal, just because you wonder about things too much.'

'I'm happy because thinking about what I might have done made me remember that lass who nearly got me to church before I'd grown up enough to make my own decisions. Mabel Watkins. I saw Jim the other day. The one who didn't get away. He looked very, very, supernaturally clean. And the most miserable looking bugger you'll see between here and Barnsley.'

'Weren't he in Bernard's junior band? Aye, he bloody were. His embouchure were never right so Bernard tried him on drums then 'ad to let him go. He cried. Jim, not Bernard.'

Stirling tipped his glass to drain the last mouthful and stood up. Hardly unsteadily at all. 'Come on. I can hear Bernard telling us off from 'ere. Takes me back to being in his junior school band meself.'

Horny was still smiling as he and Stirling tiptoed carefully into the band room. Tiptoeing proved to be unnecessary, as the tuning-up din was tremendous.

Bernard tapped his stick on his stand and glared at them. 'Good of you two to come at all,' he said with an attempt at silky menace which emerged as elderly petulance. 'Now we're all here at last, gentlemen, let me have your thoughts on the theme for the concert which we have been invited to give at the opening of our new village hall. Have you considered the subject?'

Stirling looked at Horny.

'What were it? Can you remember?' he whispered.

Horny pointed with his instrument at Bernard.

'You will remember that I asked you to work on the idea of new lives, new beginnings, and suggested we get up part of Dvorak's *New World Symphony*.'

'Why didn't you say? Bloody 'ell,' Stirling muttered. 'I could have thought about it.'

'What difference would it have made?' Horny answered. 'Anyroad, I got your answer. How did it go? "I'll join the legion, that's what I'll do..." ' His voice deepened to a melodramatically rich baritone as he sang and he half rose, putting a theatrical hand on his breast,

' "Goodbye, goodbye, we wish you all a last goodbyeeee..."

'Oh, yes. Sorry, Bernard. No, we're not going. We're ready.'

Overture

Night. The concert was over and Stirling was about to get into bed.

In spite of being grandly titled "New Beginnings" the concert had gone much as usual. Stirling had sat in his usual chair with Horny, the band's solo horn player and his oldest friend, on his right. Then there'd been the usual drinks around the usual table in the pub and Horny had seemed the same as usual but he wasn't. Stirling knew. But he couldn't work out why.

He stood and scratched his belly and his backside in a thoughtful and detailed way for several minutes, then climbed into bed, resolved to puzzle out what was wrong with Horny before he fell asleep.

But tonight Dolores had been dreaming. Her favourite dream. In the dream Dolores was running away down the crowded streets of Huddersfield, pursued by George Clooney. Dolores was only running because she had been brought up by magazines which told young girls to be sure not to give in too easily. George was calling after her, as he always did, telling her that he liked small square middle-aged women with unusual names. When she thought she'd made him wait long enough she turned into his waiting arms.

That the arms happened to be Stirling's was routine, and Stirling forgot his problem about Horny.

Horny's bedroom window, just a few houses down the street from Stirling's, was open. The April night was silent until cats started revelling nearby and an owl hooted on its way to the moors beyond.

Horny lay staring wide-eyed and sightlessly at the grey ceiling. He didn't hear the cats or the owl. He was thinking about Annie.

New beginnings, he thought. The right words for how he felt. Usually he enjoyed the atmosphere, the feel of the instrument in his hands and against his lips, Stirling grumbling on his left, familiar attempts at control from Bernard who had been bossing the band since Horny was seven. But now Annie's face, in the forefront of his mind, made him impatient with the old ways.

He'd tried to shift the face, the smile, the eyes. He'd tried to jostle it out of the way with memories of other faces, old girl-friends, and there'd been plenty, some sexier, many more beautiful, but Annie's quiet face went on smiling at him …

It was a month later. Five days before Whit Friday.

'… so have a good rehearsal but don't be late. You know me mother's coming for …'

Stirling grunted and pulled the door shut behind him. He stood on the single step, as he always did, and looked first up the street – yes, Billy at the end was polishing his Fiesta – then down the street. Only a cat walking with wary dignity and tail held up like a majorette's baton. No Horny. He threw an automatic glance towards the moors which concluded his street as they concluded every street in Harden Moss. Nice day, they told him. Finally he looked up at the aeroplane which droned directly above him on its flight path to Manchester airport.

'Poor buggers. Home from Greece. Unless they're Greeks on their way to the shores of the Manchester Ship Canal. Still poor buggers, then. Aye, well. Better get on I suppose,' he murmured, stepped down and walked past three other grey stone terrace houses, taking in familiar Sunday morning information: early roast lamb smell at number 26, late breakfast smell at 24 and raised voices at 22. No sounds, no smells, no evidence of life at 20.

Stirling knocked.

Where the bloody 'ell is he? thought Stirling as he tried to find a comfortable place for his shoulder on Horny's wall. Late, that's where. I knew he'd be bloody late.

'Bloody late again,' he muttered as he shifted from one shoulder to the other three minutes later.

'You're bloody late again, lad,' he said aloud as the door beside his shoulder opened a crack and Horny sidled through. Stirling had a brief glimpse of soft, white, drifting cloud-like cloth behind him as the door whispered languorously closed.

'Even when we've got a bloody Sunday morning rehearsal you're late,' he continued to Horny's back. 'And who were that in thy house?'

'Get a move on, Stir. You know what Bernard's like. And he's mad keen on us doing well at Whit Friday. I don't know why he thinks we will. We never have.'

'Hey, lad. Hang on. Whose bloody fault is it we're late? Whose bloody fault has it been that we've been late for everything, all us lives? Bloody 'ell. Forty year ago, first day at school, we was late.

'Me mam never wanted me to play with you, you know,' he puffed.

Horny stopped suddenly and Stirling almost collided with him.

'Hello, love. Haven't seen you for – oooh – too long.' The voice was husky and soft.

Stirling peered past Horny's broad back. A woman was looking up at Horny, high heels thrusting her body eagerly forward, eyes wide, damp mouth ajar, smiling.

What is it about you, lad, Stirling thought to himself. Ordinary looking, greyish brownish hair, what's left of it, no taller than the rest of us, nothing flashy about you – he looked at what Horny was wearing – an old pair of jeans and an old grey sweater – and the birds just fall over each other to get to you. All right, so you've not got quite my comfortable shape, but then you haven't got our Dolores' cooking every night. Meat and potato pie, eh? Stirling's thoughts hazed into happy sensations.

He came to suddenly. Horny was edging past the woman, moving on up the road, muttering excuses. The woman looked bemused. Her face held the blankness of shock. She tottered a little as she teetered on her way.

'Are you all right, lad?' Stirling asked anxiously, catching Horny and walking alongside him. 'There's summat bloody up with thee. That's the first time I recall you giving up the chance to sweet talk a reasonable-looking woman.'

Horny looked away from Stirling and up towards the moors which formed the skyline at the top of the road up to the bandroom. It seemed as though he was going to say something then he gave up.

'I've … err … '

He stopped again then tried again. 'There's something I've got to … err …'

Stirling was beginning to be worried. He grabbed Horny's sweater and pulled him round so that they were face to face.

'Don't look so bloody shifty, lad. You've done summat, haven't you? What?' He shook the sweater.

'It's just … There's a difference in my life, in a sort of way …'

Horny stopped trying to talk, yanked his sweater out of Stirling's grip and strode on.

Stirling almost broke into a run. Last night's fish and chips got in the way. He shouted instead.

'Horny. Wait on.'

He was walking ahead with his back towards Stirling. Stirling could see the red creeping round his neck and recognised it.

'Spit it bloody out, lad. We'll sort it, whatever it is.'

'It's just that there's a change, like.'

'You said that already. What?'

'Just something ... new ...'

'New job, eh? Well, no surprise there. You've had fifteen jobs to my one.'

'No, it's … err … More important, like.'

'You're not ill, are yer?'

The head turned away from Stirling shook from side to side, silently. The crimson continued to spread and deepen.

Stirling stood still. The solemnity of the next possibility which occurred to him was too enormous to allow him to say the words and move.

'Horny. You're not leavin' the band.'

It was a statement. Stirling could not make it a question. The idea that Horny might say yes was too terrible.

Tommy, bass trombone, as late as they were, joined them from a tributary street. Horny looked round at him with relief.

'Hey up, you two. Bernard'll be right mad with three on us late.'

His face, red and bright as an autumn moon, shone with cheerfulness.

He turned to Horny. 'Hey, Ah know thy lass's brother. Ah were in the same youth band. Must be thirty year ago. Remember him well. Spotty. Teeth got in the way of his embouchure. So you're keeping company with Annie Sutcliffe, eh, lad?'

Horny stole a quick glance at Stirling who realised that his mouth had dropped open.

Thirty years as a plumber had formed Stirling's imaginative thinking. It came to him that he had been picturing the elements of Horny's situation as lengths of pipe, irreconcilable in dimension, material and function. This lass was the flexible multi elbow joint he needed.

'Is she what all this has been about..?' he began then realised that he was talking to the backs of two men moving fast and disappearing into the band room. Stirling again tried to break into a trot and again gave up the attempt. He could hear the discordant sounds of the band tuning up, perceptibly more discordant than the sounds they made when playing.

'Not really bloody late at all!' he murmured as he climbed the three steps to the band room door.

The rehearsal progressed like all Bernard's rehearsals. As a teacher should, Bernard tried to be encouraging while showing where improvements might take place. The band did as the band always did and more or less ignored him, blowing its way through the hour and a half with stolid and stubborn inflexibility.

'Well, gentlemen,' Bernard said as he put his baton down, 'I think we can congratulate ourselves on an excellent morning's work. Now I'm looking forward to Lil's Sunday lunch and I expect you'll be wanting to get home to enjoy yours. I shall see you all tomorrow evening. And don't be late.'

'A pint is it?' asked Tommy. 'Nice day like this, why don't we go outside? You go and Ah'll bring 'em.'

'Grand,' said Stirling. 'Dolores won't expect me yet. And I've got to get me courage up. Her Sunday dinner's enough of a challenge without her bloody mother being there and all.'

'Come on, then, lad. Tell us,' he continued as he and Horny went out to the front of the pub to sit on the low stone wall. 'Is this Annie the lass I saw a bit of through your door? The bit I saw looked nice. What's the rest of her like? And why the bloody secrecy? And how come Tommy knows and I don't? I thought thee and me had mated round all us lives.'

'It's new. Like I said …'

'Several times, as I recall.'

'… and I don't feel about Annie like I did about the rest, all the girls I've been with before. It's right hard to explain, Stir. I think I needed to sort it out in me head afore I told you, since it's bound to make such a change, if you see what I mean.

'She's a person, somehow, not just a woman. Almost a friend. I feel as though I've known her as long as you. Even though it's not true, that's how I feel.'

Stirling felt a twinge. Indigestion from the fish and chips, perhaps.

'I've never felt like that about Dolores,' he said. 'She just happened to be there, one night, then another night, then stuck around until it seemed natural to get bloody wed. I can't say I've ever thought of her as a friend. Doesn't seem natural to have a woman as a friend. She doesn't understand how a man wants to carry on. She fusses over little things. You know? No, you don't. Not bloody yet.'

Three pints appeared with Tommy behind them.

Stirling scratched his head to clear it and cheered up. 'Ta, Tommy. Hey up, what are them kids doing on the green? That supposed to be bloody football? Come on, Horny, Tommy. We used to be able to play. Let's show 'em how it should be done.'

The three men took long swigs of their beer then put down their glasses and ran with three degrees of heaviness on to the stretch of grass in front of the pub.

The children with the football first showed dignified resistance to surrendering their ball then resignation then amusement before finally collapsing into helpless laughter and sitting on the grass in a raucous, ribaldly-commentating semi-circle watching three lumbering middle-aged men trying to run, falling over and tangling themselves in a series of disorganised, lumpy, writhing heaps.

'Ah didn't recall as football was this painful,' panted Tommy. 'Ah tell thee what. Let's us three play them little childer. You tell that 'un, Horny. And Stir, try to run, not waddle. We'll play down the hill. Right, lads. Let's show 'em.'

Stirling had to go on his own to the next night's rehearsal. He was about to explain to Bernard where Horny was when something gave a push to the swing door into the bandroom. A hard, roundish whitish thing appeared through the door at waist level. The band sat motionless, watching, hardly breathing. The whitish thing elongated and continued its dramatic entry, followed by the rest of Horny in a wheelchair.

Stirling glanced at Bernard's face. It was a classic mask of horror. Eyes and mouth staring wide, cheeks blanched. Then Stirling examined the wheelchair pusher. She looked embarrassed by having to face the concentrated attention of twenty-something people. She was nice, Stirling decided, round and comfortable. She was wearing just the sort of clothes which Stirling, pleased with his sophistication, decided might be chosen by a woman who was going to hospital to accompany her man having his broken leg plastered. Dolores asked him later what colour, skirt or trousers, jumper or jacket, and Stirling couldn't say. They were proper, he told her. And nice.

Stirling took this in as she was struggling to manoeuvre the wheelchair behind the back row cornets who had jumped up to help but being back row cornets found it difficult. She came breathlessly to Horny's proper place at last. She looked at Stirling as he got up to move Horny's usual chair to make room for the wheelchair.

'You must be Stirling,' she said. 'I'm Annie.'

Stirling saw the flush of self-consciousness on the broad cheeks. The eyes, a warm brown, had deep crinkle lines at the outer corners as though she laughed a lot. They looked directly into Stirling's. A few grey hairs brightened her natural brown. Her mouth was wide and she smiled at him as he helped to drag the chair into position.

'Not nice,' he said to himself. 'Lovely. Bloody lovely.'

Tommy, wearing a sling to protect his dislocated shoulder, nodded across to Horny. "How long had you to wait in the Infirmary? Didn't get home last neet till gone ten. Disgraceful, Ah say.'

Bernard spoke more loudly than any of the band could remember since their infants' school days. 'I suggest that we cancel our band bus and hire an ambulance instead to get us round Whit Friday. That is if any more of the band want to indulge in childish games. Meanwhile, if Tommy can hold his instrument, can we make a start on our rehearsal?'

March

Whit Friday. What Saddleworth bandsmen and drinkers call the greatest free show on earth. When pubs stay open all hours and only serve beer in plastic glasses. When the noblest brass bands in the world contest against school beginners. When triumph for a band depends on the skill of its coach driver almost as much as on its players. When Dukinfield and Greenfield, Uppermill and Delph, Dobcross and Ashton, Mossley and Heyrod are all glorious places, offering dreams of victory, points and money.

Every village and town hanging on to the Lancashire side of the Pennines with its fingertips hums with crowds and excitement. The policemen who stop all traffic save for the big band buses chat in their shirt sleeves with girls pushing their babies towards the streets where the bands will soon be marching, or on to the greens where the set marches will thunder for the adjudicators sweating in tiny tents or caravans, comforted by a bucket of sawdust and a couple of cans of Boddies.

Seasoned Whit Friday nighters are already sitting on folding picnic chairs with flasks and rugs ready for the long cold evening to come; police horses click haughtily towards Delph; youths who love bands only on Whit Friday nights are getting ready to cheer the big names with their plastic glasses of lager; mums and dads are planning their route from one town to the next to support their child's school band. A pale moon hangs, watching, in the clear sky.

Harden Moss Silver Band waited to set off down Greenfield main street, fingers on valves ready for their marching-up march, *Death or Glory.*

'Bloody good choice,' hissed Stirling, bending to Horny's ear as he sat in his wheel chair. 'You can see them folk are wondering which we chose!'

'You aren't helping any. Have you seen yourself? No, I don't suppose you could've,' Horny said balefully, and glancing up at

Stirling's face he winced. The splendid new glasses, bought especially for Whit Friday so that Stirling could read the notes he was supposed to play from the distance of his lyre, were a tangled knotted twisted mesh of wire balanced on his nose with only one lens and that strapped in with sellotape.

'How the bloody 'ell was I to know the bus was going to set off with a jerk like that when I was leaning out of the door? Me glasses fair jumped off me nose, then bloody great fool of a driver had to run over them, hadn't he?'

The drum struck up their marching beat and they set off. Annie, high heels clipping at double speed, pushed Horny, leg first; Stirling, head cocked on one side, stumbled along as he squinted at his music; Tommy's elbow, balanced on a makeshift platform to hold his instrument, pointed the way for them like an old-fashioned signpost.

Ripe comments followed them all down the street and Annie's face got redder and redder.

'Tha's on reet road to the Infirmary, lass. Just keep goin'.'

'Why dun't tha tek more watter wi' it?'

'Bernard been beating you up again, as 'e?'

'What did t'other band look like when tha'd done?'

Bernard was inflexible. The line of his mouth got harder and thinner as the night wore on. Lil, Bernard's wife, did her usual competent Contest Secretary's job of signing-in the band, and they played at nine contests before they were allowed a break at ten o'clock.

As they collapsed on to a low wall outside the nearest pub, Stirling looked at Annie, leaning her arms on the back of Horny's wheel chair beside him. She had long ago kicked off her high heels and borrowed a spare pair of old trainers that one of the back row cornets had brought in case his new shoes pinched. They were too big so she had padded the toes with paper towels. As the evening got colder, so that mothers put cardigans on toddlers and the policemen shrugged back into their uniform jackets, she had covered her pink jumper with Tommy's 'Security' donkey jacket with fluorescent patch. Her protective rouge and lipstick had disappeared and her pale face showed her exhaustion.

'Now then, lass,' said Stirling, 'what do you think to it all, eh?'

'Well,' and she paused for a long time, so that Horny twisted his head to look at her face. 'I'll not forget it, that's sure and certain.'

'Hey, Annie,' said Horny slightly anxiously. 'D'you remember Delph?'

She laughed. 'That's where the mounted police were, isn't it? And the kids with pea-shooters trying to get their peas into the big instruments. Little devils.'

'Did you see that Swiss band? Leather shorts? Feathers in their hats?'

'And the kids weren't aiming for the bloody trumpets there. I heard some notes played that them instruments were never intended for,' added Stirling.

'Weren't the policemen nice?' she went on. 'Did you see that one with flowers in his helmet?'

'Aye, and a bloody pint in his hand,' said Stirling. 'He's always there at Greenfield.'

'Oh, no. There's Bernard rounding us up like a bloody sheep dog at Harden Moss Sheep Dog Trials. Can you do some more pushing, lass, or shall I ask our Dolores to spell you for a bit?'

She considered and then smiled at Stirling. 'Thanks but I reckon I can manage,' she said.

Stirling squinted at her through his single lens as they got back into marching formation. Her hair straggled over the collar of the donkey jacket; her eyes were puddles of smeared mascara in her tired face.

'I was right,' he thought to himself. 'She's bloody lovely.'

Best Local

The glories and tragedies of Whit Friday were beginning to fade in the memory of the Harden Moss bandsmen.

Three weeks had passed.

Horny and Annie were still together at Number 20, Marsden Street, to the surprise of the entire village of Harden Moss. The house seemed illuminated by their happiness. The whole street seemed warmer.

Stirling and Dolores at Number 28 were discussing the Moorfield Presentation Evening, when the Whit Friday awards would be ceremonially presented.

'Nay, our Dolores. You are going to go wi' us, aren't you? Bloody 'ell, you should. Horny says Annie can't go, and we need plenty of supporters to cheer.'

'I don't think you should be too cocky about getting an award. Triumph indeed!'

Dolores, Stirling's wife, was a small, square, plain woman. She had been small, plain and oblong when Stirling first knew her and had become squarer as the years progressed. She was the fifth child of a millworker with a bitter sense of humour. His other children had been named after their grandparents, according to his wife's wishes. There was Millie and Edward, George and Elsie. When the fifth baby was born her father asked to be allowed to choose the name of the next four children, though he expressed the hope that this one might turn out to be the last. The fact that he named her Dolores may have been one reason why she was.

She was a quiet woman, partly perhaps because of her name, but determined.

'All right, Stirling. I'll come, I suppose, for the night out. Not because I think the band's going to do anything special. I'm sorry Annie's not going. I want to get to know her. She and Horny seem to be getting on well. He looks different.'

'Aye. Fatter. He tells me she cooks right strange stuff. Couldn't do with it meself. But otherwise she seems a right nice lass. I'll get us tickets on the band bus.'

The evening was well underway. The Harden Moss party had established themselves with noisy firmness around the central tables set out in the bar of the Conservative Club in Moorfield, and the President was about to start presenting the awards. He was enjoying himself. Words emerged long, fat and round, like sausages from an old-fashioned hand-cranked sausage machine.

'It gives me considerable pleasure, and, I may say, pride, as President of the Moorfield Whit Friday Band Association, to welcome such a number of ... err ... welcome ... err ... guests to hour awards ceremony.'

Not many people were listening. Most were watching how fast the beef was going. It was the President's privilege to supply the beef for the suppers at Band Association events, and it may have helped his election as President of Moorfield Whit Friday Association that he was the local butcher. The beef was always excellent. As were the teacakes, provided by the Vice President, the village baker. Sop suppers at Moorfield Band Association events were well attended. People really knew which side their teacake was sopped at Moorfield.

'We commence the presentations this year, as is hour custom, ladies and gentlemen, with the cup for best Youth Band. This year the magnificent 'Arold 'Inchliffe Cup has been awarded to ...'

'Hey up, lass. We wants us supper before next year's Whit Friday. Yon teacake's piled up wi' enough beef to feed our kid for a year. Sop it in't gravy and start pilin' mine. Ta, lass. An' pass us t'pickled onion. Ah'm partial to onion.'

Tommy sat down with his dripping sandwich beside the rest of the Harden Moss fan club.

'Tha wants to get in t'queue, tha knaws. Gravy's goin' to run out.'

'Shut thi bloody mouth on thi teacake, Tommy. We're gettin' to the Main Event,' growled Stirling.

'Now for the award of the Stanley Withington Cup and £25 for the best local band. This year two bands tied in the points. 'Arden Moss and Marsthwaite were both placed by hour adjudicator, 'oo, as you all know, is a much-respected old bandsman, 'oo formerly, in the good old days which many of us remember...'

'I can't take much more of this,' muttered Horny to Stirling. 'If he doesn't get to the point I shall explode!'

'... on one 'undred and seventy one points, which meant that that the afore-mentioned 'Arden Moss and Marsthwaite tied for 'ighest placed local band.'

'Oh, bloody 'ell,' groaned Stirling. 'Isn't old Barrel o' Beef ever going to tell us who's won?'

'Hour Committee decided therefore, with the aid of a H'Ordinance Survey map kindly supplied by Mr Conway, at the Post Office,' smiling condescendingly at Mr Conway who blushed at so much public notice, 'that the nearest band to our band room 'ere at Moorfield of those afore ...'

'Get on with it,' called someone who'd finished his supper and wanted another pint.

'Is, as I was going to say when I was so rudely interrupted ...'

'Harden Moss,' shouted Horny, with a chorus of support from the clustering Harden Mossies.

'Is, if the gentleman would allow me to finish ...'

'Still Harden Moss!' even more emphatically. 'Remember Dyke at the Albert Hall in 1966? Them what was there all knew who won, and told them adjudicators.'

'Aye, and we bloody know now,' added Stirling.

'Come on, gentlemen. We'll get nowhere if we don't let the President have his say.'

Bernard's reasonable conductor's words cleared enough air-space for the President to take off again. Red-faced and shaking a little, the Master Butcher, Never Bettered for Beef, according to the sign over his shop, made his announcement.

'With the use of a map, as I was trying to explain,' words now tumbling with no more dignity then thin slips of streaky bacon from a slicer, 'we decided that, as the crow flies, Marsthwaite are nearer and therefore should be the winners.'

Uproar. Harden Moss players and supporters rose to their feet. Every man and woman in the group was shouting and gesticulating.

Horny and Stirling, blessed with the loudest voices, could be heard above the rest.

'Bloody road to Marsthwaite winds for bloody miles ...'

'... walked the road with one of them measuring wheels and ...'

'Bloody near half a mile more. Favouritism. Should be bloody ashamed ...'

The other guests who had been welcomed by the President a few minutes ago joined in. Fun was too hard to come by to let slip a chance like this.

The Marsthwaite contingent pushed their tables aside and moved menacingly towards the enemy. Broad northern vowels issued from deep inside broad northern chests.

'Tha must be even dafter than tha looks ...'

'Nivver heeard o' such bad sportsmanship ...'

'Ought to be chucked aht of t'movement ...'

Moorfield's Whit Friday Vice-President, his long, crumbly, lined white face topped with his super-smooth brown toupee looking like a finger meringue dipped in shiny chocolate, laid a delicate hand on Lil's arm.

She swung round magnificently, whirling her handbag.

Luckily for the baker she missed him, connecting instead with the end of the trestle table which had supported the supper. The powerful downward swing of her weapon struck the board and catapulted the bowl of pickled onions which had not yet been cleared. It soared in a high, slow, breath-stopping arc and landed with magical precision and a tinny clang on the head of the plaster bust of Margaret Thatcher which had been donated to the Conservative Club (which turned an honest penny by letting its rooms for public events such as this presentation evening) by the local small traders otherwise known as the Chamber of Commerce.

An awed stillness descended for a second as everyone watched.

The stainless steel bowl arranged itself on the regal head at a slightly rakish angle so that the hawk-like features took on a bizarre rogueishness.

Vinegar flowed over the eyes, and they glinted wildly.

Rings of onion slid under the edges of the bowl like escaping curls. Lady Thatcher took on a gamey, desperate, street-walker look as an onion slice over one eye made her seem to be winking.

The President, with a thin, strangled scream of horror, lunged towards the bowl and bust which presided on a pillar, specially erected for the lady.

Unfortunately the Vice President was lunging simultaneously from the opposite side and Horny and Stirling, recognising a trophy, were approaching fast from the flanks.

Eight hands reached for the bowl. The butcher's hands though strong were too reverent and the baker's too dainty. Horny and Stirling, with a skirl of triumph, wrenched the bowl off the head which rocked and teetered for an endless second before falling into a Presidential embrace.

'Bet that took her back,' puffed Horny heavily to his neighbour, who he hadn't noticed was a Moorfield man and who hit him, hard.

'Use some respect,' the stranger said then found he had run out of air. Horny was kneeling on his chest.

It was old Walt, the committee's ancient retainer, who called the meeting to order. Shouts, insults, even blows had been flung, and everyone was tiring a little. After all, many of them were well over the hill, though whether it was to the Lancashire or the Yorkshire side could have started another argument.

Walter had smoked his pipe with quiet enjoyment throughout. Now he leaned forward and as he knocked the dottle out and blew to clear it he said, 'T'Moss mud 'ave a point.'

Combatants froze, mid-action, then sank on to the chairs and tables which were still upright. Heads swivelled towards him. A solitary beer glass rolled along across a table then fell and smashed. No one noticed.

Stirling was the first to speak.

'What did you say? That 'Arden Moss might have a point? Of course we've got a bloody point.'

'Soa tha mun tek boath Contest Seketaries into t'Committee Rooam and see if tha can't agree.'

The small procession which filed into the Conservative Club kitchen consisted of Lil, grandly dishevelled, her glorious bosom heaving in a way which the Vice President found dreadfully distracting, the Contest Secretary of Marsthwaite, a man who looked as if he had started shrivelling at thirteen and was now sixty five, the President, the bust of his adored one now apparently glued to his shirt front, and the Vice President whose wig had slid to one side of his head, so that a white stripe outlined the top of his right ear while his left side burn reached nearly to his chin. The effect was disturbing. It made him look a dangerous man, unstable, erratic, who might carry a bottle of nitroglycerine in his inside breast pocket which he was ready and willing to use.

When they had gone in and shut the door the barman who had rattled down his shutters in protest rattled them up again. After all, the Conservative Party needed the beer money. The contending factions sat agreeably together.

'Here, lad. Sup this. It'll help your chest,' said Horny companionably to the man whose ribs were still concave from his knees, then, settling himself, 'D'you know how much we've spent on trying to win the best local? Two hundred and twenty five pounds odd. In round figures we've wasted a couple of hundred quid. And that's if we win the prize money.'

' 'Ow did yer spend that much?' wheezed his neighbour.

'After we'd heard results we thought we'd done summat marvellous. A third section band drawing with Marsthwaite, first section! So we hired a surveyor to check distances and things. And it were him who said we'd a shorter road to Moorfield, and if we could just make sure that it were road distances that counted we'd be up there among the winners. And have a diddy little cup for us trophy cabinet. Us empty trophy cabinet.'

His neighbour took a long draw from his glass. 'Marsthwaite's doin' well just now. They won't begrudge you the cup. It were only the principle that made 'em fight, like.'

'Nay, lad. We won't take charity. We want to win the cup fair and square.'

'Aye,' chipped in Stirling who was now drinking his ale out of the trophy pickled onion bowl, 'an' if we can't bloody win it by playing we'll win it by bloody scrapping.'

ompromises must always be sought. Lil will even
putting a cogent case for us,' said Bernard

ase was winning the day. In the tiny Committee
n, Lil was bending low over the map, just across
President and his Vice. Her delectable bosom
ed her finger energetically along the roads between
len Moss and Moorfield. The Vice President felt
ested his steadying hand on the map he felt it warm
ingers. Warm, he realised breathlessly, because Lil
w hazy seconds ago from between her breasts. He
erfume which drifted up to him from the B roads of
d he became even more unsteady as he dreamed of
ce where those B roads had been nestling. He lost the
thread of the argument.

Lust had overtaken both dignified shopkeepers. The President
was also failing to concentrate. Margaret Thatcher's nose was making
a bruise just over the butcher's heart. He held her even more tightly.

'So there you have it,' said Lil.

The baker trembled.

'Have I won you over?'

The baker's wig slipped a little more.

'So, Stirling. What do you think? Was it worth it?' asked Horny
as the two men squeezed into the back seats of the band bus. 'It cost us
enough.'

'Aye, lad, but think of the bloody glory,' answered Stirling as he
held the pickled onion bowl stickily on his lap. 'Legendary we'll be. I
reckon that this bowl should have pride of place in our bloody trophy
cabinet, never mind the cup. And every time we win a contest we
should drink to our triumph in this.'

The disputed roads over the Pennines had probably never
carried a happier load than the singing band and its supporters.

Dolores and Annie

'Come in, love,' Dolores said with bustling warmth. 'Pity about the weather. July's often miserable, isn't it? Let's hope it's better for Sunday for Scarborough.'

'Thank you very much. It's really nice of you to ask me round. I don't feel as though I've had a chance to get to know anyone since I moved in, and that's a month, nearly,' said Annie, stepping into Dolores' narrow front hall and shaking the rain from her coat.

'Here, give me that. I'll put it in my back kitchen. And you come in and sit down. I've got the kettle on.'

Their houses were identical in layout. Annie looked with fascination at the differences between the living rooms.

Horny's, number 20, was plain and clean. His living room held a scrubbed deal table, four old pine dining chairs and two wheel-backed chairs which he had told her had been his grandmother's and which stood at either side of the open fire. A mantel clock was the room's only ornament. Checked curtains hung at the tall window which looked out over much the same view as here – a narrow deep valley, the tops of trees and a road opposite leading up to the moors which circled the village. Books were piled on the wide window sill.

Number 28, where Dolores lived with Stirling, was busier. Comfortable-looking armchairs crowded the small, shiny dining table up against one wall and faced the big television set in the corner by the window. The fire was gas, simulated logs. In the alcoves on either side were shelves crammed with books, papers, photographs, a bag of knitting. The table had a bowl of fruit in the centre and there was an arrangement of flowers on the sideboard against the wall facing the window.

Dolores came back, carrying a tray of cups and plates with biscuits and a jug of coffee.

'This is very nice of you,' said Annie.

'No. I'm delighted that Horny's got himself settled. It's time enough, goodness knows. Now then ...' and she poured and Annie smiled.

An hour and a half later the women were still talking.

'You were teaching for nearly twenty years, you tell me,' said Dolores as she brought in the next jug of coffee. 'You'll miss it, you know.'

'I wake up every morning and – all right, I'm happy straight away because I've got Horny next to me, but I lie there for a moment and think 'No school.' And I'm even happier.'

'I've worked in the same shop since our Maisie were first at school and I love it. Bread and sandwiches and cakes. Them biscuits are from our shop. Go on, have another. Them's Stirling's favourites, which is one reason why he's as fat as he is. The other reason's me meat and tatie pie.'

Dolores sat back in her chair, looking complacently at her guest.

'I'm really glad Horny's fallen for somebody nice. Sensible, you know. Not a flighty dolly bird.'

Annie laughed. 'Nothing flighty about me. Horny's talked to me about his old girlfriends, and jobs. He's been restless, hasn't he?'

'It's only Stirling and the band, I suppose, that have been the steady part of his life. He and Stir started school together, Bernard set the band up because them two and their mates were such little devils for him at school and they've sat together on solo horn and flugelhorn chairs almost ever since.'

'My brother played cornet when he was young, but I've never really had anything to do with a band myself. Do you play, Dolores?'

'Me?' Dolores laughed. Annie thought she could hear an edge of bitterness beneath the laughter. 'No. Never had the time or the talent. And the men'd rather be on their own. Besides.' She stopped, then went on, 'I've got used to having evenings to meself.'

'Don't you go with the band to concerts and contests, then?'

'I'm nearly always in the club on a Saturday night when they're playing. That's quite nice. And there's not usually anything I fancy on telly, Saturdays.'

Dolores reached over and took another biscuit. She ate it slowly and had finished chewing before she spoke again.

Annie waited quietly.

'Having a bandsman in your family is a funny thing. It changes as you go on. When you're a young lass the band is just noise and rough talk. It seems really clever to be the girlfriend of one of them bright ones up on the stage. Then when you're stuck in the house night after night with a kid, and you're always on your own, then ...'

She broke off. 'Not that I mind him being out.'

She got up. 'It's my own fault. I've never been one for making a lot of friends.'

She started to carry the tray into the back kitchen.

Annie rose, too, sorry and unable to say so. She followed Dolores.

'Thank you very much for being so kind to a stranger,' she said, a little awkwardly. 'Will you come down to our house next? I can't go to Scarborough on Sunday, so maybe we'll have a bite of tea instead, since you said you're not going, and perhaps you can tell me more about the band and our men folk.'

Her last words hung in the air as a question as she pulled on her coat and stepped out into the sheeting Pennine rain.

Playing in the Park

Sunday and the rain had cleared. The air sparkled, freshly rinsed and drying in a brisk wind.

The Harden Moss Band Bus waited patiently outside the band room.

Bernard the conductor stood nervously beside the driver.

Together they watched as the band arrived, nearly all portly men, smart in their maroon walking-out jackets and grey trousers.

'Funny thing,' said the driver, 'how the biggest instruments come in the littlest cars.'

He nodded towards Reg who was struggling to extract his E flat bass in its massive case from the back seat of his two door Metro.

'By 'eck, bloody thing's bigger than the car!'

'Come on, gentlemen,' Bernard called anxiously to the stragglers. 'The job starts at two, remember, and we can't afford to be late.'

Four hours to get to Scarborough, he calculated for the hundredth time. Then we've got to allow at least an hour to find Peasholme Park, and set up. My goodness, I'm nervous, but it's a real honour for Harden Moss Band to be asked to play on the island. I well remember seeing John Fosters Black Dyke Mills Band there. The name rolled its majestic length in his mind.

He smiled.

'What's up with you, Bernard? What's so funny?'

A sharp voice scratched the old-fashioned long play record which was Bernard's memory and he jumped.

'Thinking, was you? Remembering something nice? You can tell me all about it when we're on us way. It's time we set off, or hadn't you bothered to work out how long it'll take us?'

A head, built upon with an edifice which Lil called her Spring Bonnet, withdrew carefully into the bus. Bernard saw the massive shape dominate the front seat.

The bus driver considered him kindly as they got in.

'Come and sit here next to me, mate, so we can discuss the

route,' he suggested.

Bernard looked at him gratefully. 'Thanks, but I'd better sit with my wife,' he said.

Scarborough was bright but the wind was stronger here, and off the sea, and the air was shivering.

Horny and Stirling puffed along steadily at the back of the line of bandsmen taking their instruments through the park towards the bandstand on the platform in the middle of the lake.

'What's that bloody thing ... the dragon's got on her head?' asked Stirling. 'Copy of ... puff ... Huddersfield Town Hall? ... Just about ... bloody big enough.'

'Bit too wide for that. More like the station. Hey, look at that, Stir. It nearly escaped. She needs both hands to keep it from flying away.'

'With a bit of luck ... puff ... it'll take off and she'll go with it. ... Bloody hell ... It shines when it catches the sun. Look ... puff ... It's all covered with feathers. It's like a flock of bloody pigeons ... sitting on top of the Town Hall. Or the station.'

'Come on, Stirling. Stop gassing. They're getting into the boats. We shall have to swim if we don't look sharp.'

They broke into a very moderate jog.

'Forget swimming. Synchronised bloody sweating, this,' panted Stirling.

The afternoon wore away gently. From a distance, at any rate. And most people seemed to stay at a distance.

Bernard was really almost proud of his musicians. They had had no access to alcohol, were slightly nervous at the thought of the return journey across the Peasholme Park Lake and even the likes of Horny were in awe at the thought that they were sitting on the very chairs which had supported the ample behinds of Copperworks, Brighouse and Faireys, so they were unusually docile.

As he wagged his baton feverishly for the finale, '1812', Bernard caught Lil's eye and he dared to be the first one to smile. She smiled graciously back. Even from a distance he could see that she was content. A boatman had ferried her as a favour across to the island, so that she could watch the band from her own special vantage point, she looked queenly in her gold suit with the fake fur collar and her hat was triumphant. Bernard saw with fascination the complacent expression on her face as she patted its swirling stiff net outworks.

The band clattered its way to what should have been the crashing finale. Bernard bowed deeply and waved the band to their feet to acknowledge the applause from the audience of five: two mothers with prams, an elderly lady with a walking stick and a small old man with a small old dog. The dog looked the most enthusiastic.

'Let's see how quickly we can be off in the bus. There's a good drinking Sunday left,' said Reg who supervised setting up and breaking down. 'Horny and Stirling, since it looks like you're going to be the last again you can help with the timps. Be careful getting them into the boat.'

'Would be our job,' grumbled Horny mildly. 'Last back to the bus as usual. Come on, Stirling. You'd better help us lift the drum into the boat. Is that everything? Everybody? Right, then, gondolier. Let 'er rip.'

The last of the flotilla of small pleasure boats which were Dunkirking the bandsmen back to the safety of Sunday afternoon Scarborough jerked towards the landing stage while Horny and Stirling sang Speed Bonny Boat, then roared into Pratty Flowers.

They were so much enjoying their loud harmonising that they failed to hear Lil screeching at them to wait. She had wandered off to the other side of the island while the dismantling work was being done and had caught the top of her hat in the branches of a tree. It took time to untangle, and when she hurried back to the point of the island which overlooked the band's playing platform she saw that it was empty. All she saw were the broad backs of Horny and Stirling sitting side by side in a boat which was rocking a steady course away from her. She had been abandoned.

'Bernard!' she screamed out of habit, but Bernard was waiting for her on the bus, chatting to the driver.

Then she saw the canoe.

'Come here!' she yelled, and the boy in it, who had his own terrifying mother, steered it automatically towards her.

'Help me in!' she ordered.

'But you can't ...' the boy began to protest.

'Shut up and help me in!' she repeated.

And this was the scene which Stirling and Horny described later to the other bandsmen: Lil, broad and violently lurid in gold, forcing herself down into the second seat of a canoe behind a young boy, her golden thighs straining to fit inside the fibre glass. Like a cork being forced into a bottle. Then the over-loaded canoe set off. What happened was as inevitable as a Greek tragedy. Horny and Stirling certainly wept as they told it.

Lil's hat, as she sat in the canoe, was an extraordinary sight.

'Like Sydney Opera House on top of Harden Moss moor,' as Horny explained.

'Aye, and she were holding on that tight to the bloody canoe that the hat had to take care of itself,' added Stirling, 'so when the first bloody breeze came it went!'

They saw Lil's face, a mask of horror and despair, and they saw the small old dog regain its lust for life as it ran into the water and paddled for the hat, now floating arrogantly like a multi-coloured swan.

Lil screamed and leaned over to try and reach the hat first.

Then everything happened in classic slow-motion: Lil's arms flew up, her mouth opened wider than possible, though no sound could yet be heard, the canoe began to roll and Horny's flat and Stirling's fat bellies hit the lake in an explosive parting-of-the-waters-type plunge. As lads they had learnt to swim together at the old Ramsden Street Baths in Huddersfield.

'I told you we'd have to bloody swim for it,' jerked Stirling.

'Shut thi face. Just swim,' panted Horny.

When they reached it the upside down canoe was bouncing with the panicky movements of Lil. The lad had eeled his way out, but she fitted that canoe.

Horny and Stirling dived, yanked, strained, pulled, ripped out hair, cloth and finally Lil herself. She was a floppy mass of sodden gold and fur. But she was still spluttering 'Bernard.'

They dragged her to the island's jetty and pumped some of Peaseholme Park Lake out of her.

'Lil!' screamed Bernard's voice from the bank, and he and the remaining twenty three members of the band, like lemmings, dived into the water. The bus driver, who'd brought the bus up to the park, watched.

'Tsk,' he tutted, remembering how smart they had looked that morning

But the band were having a wonderful time.

'Best day out in years,' spluttered Reg. 'D'you reckon they'll ask us back?'

Music

The band bus was crawling home along the M62. Everyone had dried off, the excitement was over and Stirling was bored.

'Hey, Horny. You know our Maisie's little lad? He's bloody wick. He came out yesterday with 'What made you start to play in a band, Grandad?' And he's only five, you know.'

'What did you say?'

'Summat about having nowt else to do.'

They sat silently for five minutes while the bus progressed a dozen yards.

'What would you have told 'im about what made you start then?' Stirling asked Horny, after trying and failing to find something interesting in his newspaper.

As he often did, Horny sat and thought for so long that Stirling forgot the question and was starting work on the paper's crossword.

'What do you call a …?'

'It was Bernard started the band because we were such pains in his backside at school. He was trying to start something he could use to blackmail and bribe us with.'

'Aye. I know. I know. We all know that. It worked. What do you call a …?'

'But that doesn't explain why we kept on with it. I don't think you'd have been as bothered about the band if I'd not been fussed, would you?'

Stirling had stopped listening. He was filling in one of the words in the puzzle.

Horny leaned his head back and talked his thoughts.

'I never had anything I really cared about when I was a kid. I never took to collecting racing cars or Airfix models or Meccano. Remember Meccano, eh? Any road, we hadn't the money to buy toys. And television was always on loud in our house and I got to hate it. Noise. Smiling faces with nowt real behind the smiles. No honesty, it seemed to me, even as a kid, though I couldn't have told you that in them days. Then Bernard started the band.'

'Do you know another word for ...?'

'It seemed to matter. It seemed real. Blowing and getting a sound which fitted with everybody else's sounds. It was fantastic. And all the sounds together making a piece. I'd find myself blowing in my head at night, Stir. I've never told you that. Not practice, not playing on my trumpet, just thinking blowing. Hearing what I'd been playing at rehearsal but hearing it perfect. Beautiful.'

Horny sat in silence. His face was shining.

'What the bloody 'ell are you looking so cheerful about?' asked Stirling. 'At this rate it'll be well after eleven when we get home and pub'll be shut.'

'I reckon it changed my life, you know.'

'What? Oh, the band. And mine. Always taking up valuable drinking time, like now.'

'It's been about adding value, I reckon.'

Horny glanced at Stirling. His lips were moving as he bent over the crossword.

'Seems to me music's about important things. Somebody's written a piece which tries to explain what he's learnt about life, whether it's funny or sad. And we try to take them dots and blow sounds which get as near as we can make 'em to the composer's feelings.

'When I started playing properly it was a way into another life for me. A better one, really. Where there's harmony and peace and excitement and I can share it with twenty odd other blokes who feel the same. Well.' He glanced at Stirling again. 'Nearly all of them. Some are so brain dead that they're just there for the exercise and the thirst!'

The bus lurched a few yards. Stirling looked up.

'Are you still on about the band? Bloody 'ell. I always thought there was something funny about you.'

Widget's Concert

Two weeks vanished.

The knock on the door had been repeated by the time Dolores reached it.

'Fancy anybody calling at this time on a Monday,' she muttered as she squeezed past the pile of washing in the hallway.

She opened the door.

'Oh, it's you, our Josie' she said coldly.

'Can I come in, Auntie Dolores? I just want to explain about Widget.'

'Well ... you'll have to excuse the mess. It's only just gone nine, after all. And it's my morning off for housework,' said Dolores as she led the way along the narrow hallway to the kitchen. 'I suppose you'll have a drink of tea, will you?' she asked

'No, don't bother. I won't keep you. I wondered if you'd heard.'

'Heard? The whole of West Yorkshire'll have heard I should think. Stirling couldn't sleep. One minute he was groaning and the next he was laughing so hard I thought he'd have a heart attack.' At the memory the hard lines of her mouth softened a little.

'You weren't there, were you? No. I remember. You were baby-sitting for your Maggie. It's happen as well.'

'Go on, then. You'd better sit down. And I will put the kettle on. Here. You can make yourself useful. Fold these while you're talking.'

'It was an important concert, Auntie Dolores. Widget got himself into a real fuss about it.'

'I can guess. Widget the fidget they call him, don't they?'

'Oh, that's a bit mean. But he does take his position as top man seriously, you know. And he had me pressing his trousers and his tie three times...'

Stirling knocked on the roof of Horny's garden shed that evening as he simultaneously pushed open the door.

'That door's nobody's fool,' he said. 'It recognises me. Starts opening when I get near. How did you bloody train it?'

'Uneven ground. Enough weight and it shifts. You've come to talk about door construction, have you?'

'If you like. Probably more worth while than discussing that concert and our fool of a top man. Tomorrow night's committee meeting should bloody sort 'im.'

'Be fair, Stirling. It were a farce before he did owt. I mean, have you ever heard the band play worse? Back row cornets were even more diabolical than usual, trombones come in spare in first piece, Bernard lost control and I hadn't a clue where we were in the *Walk in the Black Forest*, that lad who stood in for Tim hasn't a sense of rhythm ...'

'Happen that's why 'e's a bloody drummer.'

'... and he set all the bass end rocking ...'

'Aye. He may not be able to beat in time but 'e's bloody loud.'

'... and I think Bernard gave up the fight in *Light Cavalry*.'

Stirling sat down emphatically on his usual pile of sacks.

'I can't deny it were a bloody mess. Did you tek note of Ticker's euphonium solo? There were that much tremolo the instrument sounded like nowt so much as a lad wi' 'is voice brekkin'. And bloody worried about what the 'ell's happening to 'im that 'e 'asn't got a clue about.'

'Yes, Stir. And every borrowed man blobbed, not just the drummer. I'm amazed that the audience stayed and didn't walk out from pity because they couldn't bear to watch grown men making such fools of themselves.'

'They bloody would ha' done if t'mayor and 'is gold chain 'adn't been there. I'm surprised t'mayor didn't walk out hisself.'

'They make sure he can't, Stir. They put him in the middle of a row with infirm old ladies on either side of him. He's programmed to applaud. That's why they have him. And what's more he goes to so many concerts and whatnot that he learns not to listen, so he didn't know how awful it were.'

While Stirling and Horny were talking in Horny's shed Dolores was entertaining Widget's Josie.

'I'm a bit sorry I was hard on you this morning,' Dolores said to her guest as she passed her a plate of chocolate digestive biscuits. 'Go on, have another. I brought two packets back from the shop.'

'Thanks ever so, Auntie Dolores. You weren't hard. You were upset, that's all. And then I got upset and we never got round to sorting things out. I'm really anxious that you should understand. I know how much Stirling relies on you.'

Dolores smiled. 'Perhaps he does, more than he thinks. Go on, then. Finish your story.'

'Poor lad came home in a right state. He had the mask with him because he's going to start doing children's entertaining. He got the idea from that Brassed Off.'

'Never saw it myself,' interrupted Dolores with conscious superiority. 'Isn't it about a girl flugel player?'

'Yes, that's right. But it's good.'

What were you wanting me to pass on to Stirling?'

'Just how sorry he is, and how he wishes he hadn't had this moment of madness.'

'So you reckon the hopeless piss-up the band put on excuses Widget, do you?'

'I'm just saying I can understand what drove him to it. Nothing more than that.'

'What I can't get me 'ead round is 'ow come 'e 'appened to 'ave that bloody thing with 'im. Do you carry a party mask? Mebbee when you do get into t'garden you slip on your Charlie Dimmock head. Eh?' Horny grinned. 'It's not Charlie's head that most people are interested in, Stir. But I agree with you. It was a funny thing to have with him, on stage, for a concert.'

'And then, to stand up there, in the middle of *Bells Across the Meadow*, as gentle and sweet a bloody piece as you're likely to find, when it's played reasonably well, that is, in full view of the mayor and corporation of Kirklees, and point to this bloody great plastic knife through 'is skull and yell 'All right, 'oo threw this?'

Stirling started to shout with laughter. 'I wish I'd been in the bloody audience.'

'It woke the mayor up, anyroad. Widget were pointing straight at him, shouting 'Did you throw this? Eh?' What were it 'e said next, summat about us working hard?'

'Aye. That's right. 'E said, 'We come 'ere, after workin' a week, an' blow our guts out for you,' still pointing to the mayor, 'and you show what you think about us by attacking us like this.' ' Stirling had rolled off his sacks by this time and was lying on his side beating his hand on the floor, 'then 'e sat down and picked up 'is instrument.'

'It were dead silence for what seemed like a full minute, Bernard hadn't any idea of what to do, he looked as if he was going to cry, then the mayor started giggling and applauding ...'

'Well, whether 'e were programmed to applaud or not, it made everybody else start clappin' and the whole of Dewsbury Town 'All fell about, laughin' so much they were bloody crying. It broke the horror of the concert, right enough.'

'And we played reasonably well after, so I don't see that the committee should sack Widget. He turned a nightmare into fun. And you're always saying, Stir, that music should be fun.'

'Right enough. It's fun to remember. Bloody terrifying to live through. We should just give 'im a warning. 'appen.' Stirling climbed heavily to his feet. 'Anyroad, I bet we get a full 'ouse next time we play in Dewsbury. Come on. I'll treat thee to a pint, just for once.'

Dolores was waiting when Stirling got home. He was very late.

'Oh, 'ello, love. Nice to see you still up. Me an' ...'

'You don't need to tell me. You and that Horny were getting yourselves sloshed. I've been talking to Josie.'

'That's nice. Nice lass is Widget's Josie. Kind, like. Gentle.'

'You wouldn't have called her kind and gentle if you'd heard what she's been saying tonight. She - and me - we're determined. We're going to make sure you take action.'

'What are you talking about, love? What do you want me to do? I know that bloody toilet door needs another 'inge, but ...'

'Really, Stirling, try to be sensible. You are going to make the committee pass a vote of censure on Widget, and suspend him for the next three concerts.'

'But ... but ... me an' Horny've come to us own decision ...'

'Well, you can just undecide it. Goodnight.'

So Widget's Josie got to take the two weeks' holiday on Gran Canaria which she had won. With Widget to carry the cases and buy the meals and drive the free hire car and rub oil into her back and ...

Surfing Stirling

'It's for you, Bernard,' Lil screeched up to Bernard in his study. 'Summat about band and sea-side.'

Bernard tumbled out of his reverie and down the stairs into reality. They were surprisingly similar.

'Could you possibly help us out, d'you think? Brighouse must obviously accept such a prestigious invitation to play at the awards ceremony, no matter how last minute the notice is, and really we're desperate,' his caller concluded. 'I can't tell you how grateful … You are our last resort, if you'll forgive the pun.'

Bernard contained his delight with some style.

'I shall obviously have to consult with my bandsmen, but if, as you say, you can cover loss of wages for the Friday and the Monday I think it likely … That's all I can say at the moment. We happen not to have a concert booked for the weekend you are speaking of.'

A short late summer venues tour. For Harden Moss Silver Band, indeed, playing at bandstands and open air locations around the south west, a luxury coach already hired, hotels booked, and refreshments free.

'What didst tha say, Bernard?' enquired a chorus at the beginning of the next rehearsal. 'Free beer? And two days' pay covered?'

'Bloody 'ell,' added Stirling, and then with a child-like need to be reassured that Christmas was definitely on its way, 'And tha didst say no wives?'

The Ocean View hotel was splendidly high over a surfing beach in Newquay.

The band played a noisy wake-up lunch-time spot for stag night professionals and other serious drinkers on the lawns in the centre of the town, then were free until their evening booking.

Tommy, Reg, Widget, Horny and Stirling joined a greenish group of student types who had cowered during their concert in the quietest free corner they could find.

'Hey up, you lot, what's to do around here?' asked Reg. 'For a group of mature men, Ah mean.'

One of the young men slanted a glance at his neighbour then said, 'Surfing's for everyone. They say it's a doddle. We're beginners, really ... err ... we've just joined a class. Why don't you come with us? But didn't you say you're from Yorkshire? I suppose it might be a bit difficult for you then.'

Half an hour later ...

'Suck it in, mate,' advised the Australian instructor who was trying to fit Stirling with a wet suit.

'It's tekken me years and a lot of bloody money to get to this shape. It's comfortable. I like it,' said Stirling. 'I don't want to tek any risks with it.'

'Don't worry. It'll still be there when you finish. Come on. No, don't breathe yet. Just the zip up the back now. Heave, ye-e-e-s. I had doubts for a moment, but we've made it. Is the oxygen still getting through? Good on yer.'

The early afternoon was grey and cloudy, soothing to eyes which found it difficult to open at all after a joyous long night's drinking but a piercing sun was threatening to break through as Stirling, Horny and the others were marshalled by three instructors whose wash board stomachs were visible even through their wet suits.

'Bye bloody 'ell. Is one of these things supposed to carry my weight?' puffed Stirling as he and Horny marched together down a cliff path, carrying two surf boards between them.

The bay beneath them was enormous, and so were the waves, to Stirling's view. Both wet beach and waves were beginning to shine in the sun.

'Right, mates. We're going to jog across the sands. Get our body temperatures up before we go in that lovely surf,' said the instructor in charge of the bandsmen.

They jogged, slowly.

'That's enough exercise for one bloody day,' Stirling gasped. 'I'll never get enough puff back to blow to-neet. Not with this thing this tight, anyroad.'

'Stretch, now. Bend each knee in turn. You need to be flexible.'

'What? Nivver. Us plumbers use elbow joints. Not bloody natural for a plumber to be flexible.'

'Balance. Now lift each foot up against your backside. Like this.'

'Urgh. Bloody urgh.'

'Arms above your head. Swing to left, right. Windmill your arms. Get up, Stirling. You can do it,' said the instructor.

Stirling looked towards the sea. Huge mountains of waves were piling up. He saw a tiny figure buried as one rolled and crashed, then the figure was beyond the great wall of sea and standing, riding the water, or so it seemed.

'Come on, mates, lie face down on your boards ...'

'That's more like it,' grunted Stirling.

'... and swing your arms as though you're paddling.'

Stirling thought he felt the thud of the next wave as it landed on the sand twenty yards in front of him.

'Right, mates. Spring up. On to your board, Stirling. And I said spring, not lumber. You look like an out-of-condition bear.'

'Horny, I can't do this,' muttered Stirling.

'So let's have a go, guys. Carry your boards.'

The sand was silkily desirable under Stirling's feet. He didn't want to leave it.

'Bloody 'ell. What 'ave I said I'd do?' he groaned.

'Come on. The water's lovely. Warm until January. And look, there's the sun.'

The sun ripped into last night's hangovers and the group now groaned as one. Even the white of the waves as they crashed was dazzlingly painful to Stirling. A sea-gull screamed with laughter above his head.

'Come on, mates. Step through these tiddlers. There's some big beauties coming up. Jump. Oh, dear, mate.'

Stirling collapsed under the weight of a two-foot wave. He spluttered to his knees.

'The water's not cold?' he said. 'Just wait until it trickles down the back of thy bloody neck, lad. Like a bloody leak from a cold water system when t'pipes have burst.'

Then he gave up protesting, lay down on his board and started to paddle out over the tiddlers towards the whales.

An hour later, Horny, Reg, Tommy and Widget sat on a wall at the top of the beach. They were watching Stirling. He was far out, in the middle distance. They could see his head and shoulders then as a wave approached from behind him he swam into it, swung his board and paddled along the crest. As it reared before breaking he stood half-crouching, fat, black and shiny as a performing dolphin and rode along the clear high green side of the wave just below its mane of foam before turning beachwards and skimming to a point where he could step off into a few inches of water.

The four watchers were silent. Their mouths still hung open.

'He's not built for it. He's not top-heavy, he's belly heavy. He shouldn't be able to balance on one of them boards,' said Tommy at last.

They watched as Stirling swung into and across another wave.

'It's not as if he's got a natural sense of rhythm. I've sat next to him in the band for forty years so I should know,' said Horny.

Stirling performed a graceful full three hundred and sixty degree turn as he slid on to the following wave.

'He's riding that wave as smooth as one of thy trombone glissandos, Tommy,' said Widget.

The shiny black figure topped the following peak like a fat mackintosh-clad fairy on a Christmas tree.

'Seein' him there standin' top o' that bloody great wave, 'e looks as steady as old Bernard's bandroom metronome,' put in Reg.

'I make no doubt he'll be auditioning for Baywatch soon,' said Horny, yawning.

After what seemed to the watchers like several more hours, Stirling waddled jubilantly up the beach, carrying his board like a glorious triumphant shield. They could hear him from some distance singing, 'I am sur - fing, I am surf - ing,' to the tune of *I Am Sailing*.

'There'll be no stopping him tonight. He's playing a solo an' all,' said Horny. 'It'll be *Fantasia on British Sea Songs* he'll be pushing for next, just you watch.'

'Right. All together, lads,' said Reg, and the waiting group sang in deep and menacing voices the theme tune from *Jaws*.

Dolores' Revenge

'Stirling,' said Horny as he put their next pints down on the table after one Thursday night's rehearsal in September, 'how's Dolores?'

'What d'ye mean, Horny? Same as bloody usual. Why?'

'Well, it's just that ...' Horny took a long pull from his glass then sat silent for a time. He started again. 'When Bernard told you you were being moved to first horn out of the flugel seat for a while, just to try it, what did you say?'

'I don't bloody remember. Summat like 'Fine' then I moved. Why?'

'Well, it's just that our lass has heard that your Dolores is right cut up about it, your being demoted, like, and she's been going on, complaining that it's not fair that Matty should move straight into flugel seat without serving a kind of apprenticeship with the band. You and her haven't talked about it, then?'

'Why should we talk about it? Nowt to bloody talk about, is there? Anyway, me and Dolores never talk. I go in at night, say 'Is me tea ready?' She says 'Wash yer 'ands an' it'll be on t'table,' then when I'm gettin' ready for practice I say to 'er "Ave I got a clean shirt?' an' she says 'In't top drawer,' an' that's it. Never bloody varies. All we ever say. Any road up, it's only a trial, in't it? I'll mebbe be back t'other side of you in a week or two.'

'You've not noticed any changes at home, then?'

'Me bloody tea's been terrible, if that's a change. No meat and tatie pie for, oh, days. Nowt else unusual. Though now you come to mention it she's been lookin' sort of red in the face. Mebbee like she'd been crying, I suppose. I'd not given it a bloody thought.'

'Happen you'd better. Women are funny things, you know.' Horny's face took on a softly nostalgic look. 'I used to think they needed cherishing. In me young days, that were. Before I met Annie and let her cherish me. That's what they really need, I've since decided. They need to have somebody that they can cherish.'

'Oh, aye,' said Stirling doubtfully. 'Let's get on to a subject I'm sure of. It's my round.'

When he got back to the table, as he eased himself down on to his chair Stirling said, 'I've never bloody understood women, you know, Horny. If I were cross about summat I'd find someone to be cross wi', shout at 'em then bloody thump 'em if I thought they needed it. Then I'd buy 'em a drink. Easy. Women aren't like that, are they?'

'You're going to be the one to suffer, Stirling,' said Horny thoughtfully. 'If Annie's right. And I've not known her wrong yet.'

'Suffer? 'Ow will I bloody suffer?'

'Board's suffering already, you say. It'll be bed next. I tell you, they're a different species.'

'But what the bloody 'ell can I do? If she's got some daft idea into 'er 'ead?'

'Work out some way in which she can get her own back on Matty's wife. Then she'll think it's all square.'

'But what?' Stirling's voice was desperate. 'Mrs Matty's a right clever young bugger. Dolores can't cook much, can't sew, doesn't look right good. It's your idea. Bloody suggest summat.'

Next night, Horny and Stirling thought about the problem in Horny's garden shed. They got as far as deciding that the forthcoming Band Harvest Festival would be a good place to stage the revenge, but no nearer deciding the form that revenge would take.

'But there must be something she's good at,' persisted Horny.

'She's bloody good at keepin' quiet.'

'Well, how about a sponsored silence?'

'Don't be so bloody daft. Honestly, Horny. Who else would do it? You can't 'ave a sponsored event for one participant, can yer?'

'Jam,' said Horny. 'It's a Harvest Festival. Can she make jam?'

'We had to cut the jar off the last lot before we could eat it,' said Stirling dourly. 'Then when we'd got the jar off an' washed the jam we had to saw it up into slices.'

'Cakes?' Horny saw Stirling's face and shook his head. 'Forget that. What about soft toys? Everybody loves the soft toys that come up for auction. I still remember that hippo she made for your Maggie when she were little.'

'That were a bloody bunny rabbit, you fool.'

The night of the Band's Harvest Festival arrived. The wives of the band had all by now ranged themselves on Dolores's side or Mrs Matty's side. Ranks were drawn facing each other across the band room, which although festively decked had the smell and feel of a waiting battle field. After the band's first half concert, the men all leaned on the bar nervously. The auction proceeded. The wives bought challengingly and bid offensively.

The bar's sales soared.

Bernard gathered the band together for the second half concert and conducted the familiar harvest hymns, Stirling sitting on Horny's right as his first horn while Matty sat on his left as flugel player.

Bernard was gratified by the attention he was getting. 'This eye-contact is excellent,' he confided to Widget. 'Not a man in the band tonight whose attention is wandering to the audience. My pep talks must be getting through at last.' Elated, he concluded the second half of the concert.

'If you all play as well as this, we'll have a real club-type third half.' he said to his men as he sent them off stage for the second interval. 'And my mother will have gone home by then.'

By ten o'clock, an air of decadence yellowed the atmosphere in the room. The band was playing rackety music, groups of women were challenging each other in song, tables were groaning with full and empty glasses and paper plates for the beef tea-cakes which Dolores' battalion had made and equal numbers of Cornish Pasty wrappers which had been provided by the Matty brigade.

Then Bernard, enjoying the band's undivided attention, beat them in with the unmistakable first notes of *The Stripper*.

The room quivered.

Dolores got up.

Stirling stopped playing in horror.

She stood, vibrating to the beat then slowly turned, glancing once with confident contempt at Mrs Matty. As she swung she pulled her cardigan off her shoulder then shrugged it on again. Off, on to the music's beat, then off and swirling it round her head she spread her knees and let it fly. As she unbuttoned her blouse she swung her backside rhythmically. The band sound was dwindling as half the players now sat, instruments against flaccid lips, watching. Her movements were hypnotic. Her squat square body stretched, dipped, turned, hazed by movement. She moved sensually, almost lazily, allowing herself to be carried by the sounds. She was now rotating, head thrown back, while her hands unclipped the hooks on her bra.

As she swung it before letting it go, Stirling saw her face. Triumphant. Fulfilled.

He glanced at Horny.

'Summat she's good at,' he said.

Watching the Wheat

'Bloody cheap bloody watch,' grumbled Stirling to himself.

'What?' asked Horny.

'Gone wrong. See, says eight o'clock, rehearsal start time, an' Ticker's not here. Must be wrong. I'd trust Ticker's time before clockwork any day.'

Bernard stopped shuffling the music on his conductor's stand and raised his head. 'Err ... gentlemen. I'm afraid I've got very sad news.'

He fell silent and shuffled some more.

'Gwen, Mrs Owen, rang Lil this afternoon to tell her that Ticker died in his sleep last night. From a heart attack.'

The semi-circle of men moved a little as if a cold wind had blown upon their faces.

'Bloody Ticker stopped, din't it?' Stirling murmured to Horny, then they looked at each other, both horrified at what he'd just said. 'Sorry. Mouth slips out of gear sometimes.'

'Gwen told Lil that she'd like the band to play at the funeral. I'm sure we'd be very glad to. Isn't that right, gentlemen? After all, Ticker played with us for nearly twenty years, from the time he came up to Yorkshire from South Wales.' Bernard waited for the ripple of agreeement before he continued. 'Thank you all. The funeral will be one week from today. My mother says she'll knit us all arm bands.'

The funeral director was a bandsman as his father had been before him. No one with band connections would ever think of going elsewhere than the neat, formal undertaker's shop in the main village street. He organised the day with regimental precision. The band would march in front of the coffin as it processed from the narrow terrace house where Ticker had lived and died through the village streets to the old square church. After the ceremony the mourners, still led by the band, would climb to the graveyard where Ticker would be buried.

All the hymns in church would be played by the band, 'and all of you will be there,' said Bernard with emphasis after they had planned the music, 'in full uniform and wearing caps.'

'It's only right we should see him off well. He were a real bandsman, even though he were Welsh,' said Horny to Stirling as they waited in marching formation outside Ticker's house on the day of the funeral. 'I tell you what'll be hardest. Playing by the grave side.'

'Bloody hard for 'is lad, as well. Ticker were that bloody proud of 'im. D'ye remember when the two of them played a euphonium duet at our Christmas concert? What did they play?'

'*Pearl Fishers*. Aye, Emrys is a grand lad. Pity he went back to Wales. Mind you, Point of Ayr's not a bad band. Not up to the Yorkshire standard, of course.'

'Hey up, Horny. See t'drum? T'bloody drummer's got 'is 'ook too 'igh. 'E won't see over t'top.'

The drum, swathed in blackout material which Bernard's mother had left over from the war, was being carried in the middle of the marching band by a lad from the village.

'You won't find it at all difficult,' Bernard had told him, when he pulled him in to replace Tim, the band's percussionist, who was having his appendix out. 'Just regular beats, that's all.'

'Slow march an' all. Lucky 'e's got trombones behind. They'll be able to keep him in t'road wi' their slides.'

The coffin, followed by Gwen, her son and his wife, began to move towards the church.

'Oh, bloody 'ell, Horny,' groaned Stirling as he raised his instrument to his lips. 'I hate funerals.'

The slow procession moved through sunshine blown across with brief light gusts of rain. Stirling was aware of numbers of people lining their route, bare-headed, tears sliding down faces as the band played *The Dead March from Saul*, then, as they stood by the church door waiting for Ticker to be carried in, the great old hymns which had ushered people out of this life for centuries, the glorious rolling sounds of *Oh God Our Help In Ages Past, Crimond* and *Abide With Me.*

Gwen had chosen her favourite, the triumphantly Welsh *Guide Me Oh Thou Great Redeemer* as the final hymn which would accompany her husband into church. Stirling's head rang with the words sung by Welsh voices as he played.

At the graveside, as they made ready for their final goodbye to a friend, Emrys stepped forward holding his father's euphonium.

'My da loved this piece of music. He played it as a solo at the first concert I ever went to. I think it always reminded him of Wales, and his own childhood.' He picked up the instrument and blew into the mouthpiece.

'*Watching the Wheat*', he said. 'The first verse goes:

When I was young I wandered free, like wind across the meadow

Astray among the silver wheat without a path to follow.

And wildly sang the summer bird, and gaily danced the flower,

And roving sunlight wove its dream of joys that last for ever.'

His voice faltered as he spoke the words but then the voice of the euphonium rose clear and sweet.

As Stirling played the familiar accompaniment he heard not Emrys but his father, standing in front of the band to solo in so many concerts. They'd nagged him to try other pieces, and he did sometimes, but it always seemed right when the pattern of the old notes fitted themselves into their comfortable places inside Stirling's head. Happy and sad at the same time. Like now.

Gwen stood with her head bent, eyes shut. She was remembering when she first heard this piece. It was one summer Sunday. She was only just seventeen and she and a friend had got dressed up to walk down into Pontypridd town centre. They'd heard a band and hurried to listen. She'd seen him, handsome she thought in his red uniform with gold braid. He was standing up in front of all the others to play, and he looked so important. When he finished everyone clapped, but he looked at her. Just her. Then after they'd played he came to find her.

Emrys made each note as perfect as he could. For his da. His da and he had never talked much but they had still shared all the most important things. His own life would have been a desert without music, he knew, and he knew the same was true for his da. This song held the best memories of all. He was glad he could make it a last gift. He was once again the little boy listening to his da, proud as could be, then the man in middle age, still proud of the old man as he stepped forward to play his last solo. A bit more tremolo, now, but the notes still confident and happy. He remembered his da's face when Emrys told him that he's been accepted as solo euphonium for Point of Ayr band. 'I never made it to the top rank,' he'd said. 'I'm glad that you have, lad.'

The music floated over the valley. As Bernard conducted it seemed to him that this was a perfect way to leave life. Sunshine, and friends sharing music, the soloist's notes soaring then enfolded by the warm tones of the other players. And it's been a good way to live, he thought, as his hands stroked the last notes into silence.

Stirling and Horny sat uncomfortably in Ticker's house, gripping the tiny hooked china handles of Gwen's best tea cups with thick red fingers. They were desperately uncomfortable.

'Hey up, lad. Let's go out into the garden. I can't cope wi' this,' muttered Horny.

'Too bloody true,' hissed Stirling. 'T'women love this sort o' thing. Can't understand it.'

In the little garden, leaning their backs comfortably against Ticker's shed, they stood watching. Through the polished window they could see women moving in their mysterious rituals, handing plates, pouring tea, washing dishes, generally bustling.

'Gwen's under a strain, I make no doubt, but she still looks a bloody sight better than last time I saw her,' said Stirling.

'Go on. When were that?'

'Me and Ticker'd been to Dyke's open rehearsal, a week or two back, and we'd had a couple on us way home. Then we had a couple more, because it were a bloody good pint, then just another one or two for old times' sake. It must've been gettin' on for two in the bloody mornin' or a bit later. I walked 'im 'ome. like you do when you've shared a few, an' he had all on to fit 'is key into t'bloody door. He more or less fell in, and we thought that were really funny, then he shouted ' 'Ello' in his deep Welsh voice. I told him to be quiet and said I'd better go, but he said, 'No, it's all right,' then ' 'Ello!' even louder. After he'd shouted a fair few times we heard a little voice from upstairs, 'Is that you, Ticker?' 'Aye,' he said. 'If you're awake, Gwen, you can come down and get us some supper!' An' she bloody did!'

Horny grinned. 'I like that story from when we always played *1812* at concerts, and Tommy used to let off the fireworks behind the trombones. Weren't we at the Town Hall this particular day? Aye, we were, and Tommy decided to add flares to the fireworks, without telling us, of course. People in the audience, when they could talk without laughing, said it looked grand, but Ticker with his back to the flares could only see the reflection of flames, he said, and his own shadow flickering in front of them.'

'I'll never forget it. So he did what any bloody Welshman would do, didn't he? He bloody ran. Straight across t'stage, carrying his instrument, before he realised.'

Gradually the rest of the band escaped their women and joined Stirling and Horny in the last of the sun. The wind had dropped and the late September sky was clear of clouds.

They stood, silently, watching the dark encroaching, then Horny said, 'Hey, lads, how about asking young Emrys if he'd like to come down to t'club wi' us. There's a reasonable beer on, and I'd like to buy the lad a pint. He fair did Ticker proud the way he played his tune. Reet?' and the group of gloriously dressed men put on their caps and made their final procession of the day.

Horny in the Middle

Horny was thoughtful that October. Stirling noticed nothing until one wet evening. He and Horny were having their usual après-rehearsal drinks but when Stirling came back to their table from the bar he looked down with consternation.

'Bloody 'ell, Horny. That pint's never been touched. Art ill, lad? Shall I tek this new'un and see if I can get me money back?'

Horny shook himself. 'Nay. Put it down. I ... err ... I've got summat on me mind, like.'

Stirling sat down suddenly, as though his legs had given way.

'Tha shouldn't give a man shocks like that. It's not 'ealthy.' He took a long, reassuring draw from his glass then wiped his lips with the back of his hand.

'Go on,' he said. 'I can bloody face owt now. Bad news, is it?'

'Well, it depends what you call bad news.'

'I call it bloody bad news if it comes between a man and 'is pint,' said Stirling. 'Just tell us, will you?'

'I'm thinking of ...' began Horny then stopped.

'Get on with it, you bloody great Nellie.'

'Well ... of ... having a change from playing.' Silence stretched. 'Say summat, Stirling. I've been sitting in solo horn spot for nigh on forty years.'

'An' you're still trying to decide whether or not it bloody suits you, that it?'

'It's not that simple. I fancy trying me hand at conducting.'

Stirling looked at him, awed. 'That's amazin', that. I sit on me chair and blow, an' never think about why I do it. You've been goin' away and bloody thinkin', 'aven't you?'

'Sorry,' said Horny.

'No need to be sorry. I'm impressed. It never enters me head, that's all. I suppose its like some men who 'ave these extra muriel affairs. It just would never occur to me. I can look at these bloody lovely little lasses with itsy bitsy skirts nearly down to their backsides and enjoy lookin' but the notion of mekkin' a move on one of 'em would never cross me mind. There's our Dolores at 'ome, and that's that. How my life is. Same wi' t'band. See?'

'Course I see,' said Horny, 'but this, it's like summat I really want to do. I just don't want not to ever have tried. I watch Bernard, wagging the stick, and I think I could do that. And sometimes, when we're working on a test piece, say, I feel things in the music that I want to pass on to the rest of the band.' He glanced at Stirling's open mouth and his voice trailed into silence. 'Anyway, I mentioned it to Bernard, and he seemed to think it weren't a bad idea, and he'd not mind a bit of a rest, and I'm going to conduct the next concert. Thought I'd tell you before you saw me up in the middle. Wagging.'

Stirling lay awake that night and thought for a long time. About how he and Horny had known each other from when they started school on the same day. How they'd always got into trouble together, caught their one and only stickleback, tunnelled their best den into a load of hay-bales, shared the secrets of the co-op horse and joined the band together. They'd never been the same, though. Horny'd usually led in their wildnesses, and certainly he'd been one on his own in his girl-hunting.

But this. Horny would be really alone in this. He thought about the loneliness of the man standing in the middle with his baton and shivered as he lay.

Hey! Never mind Horny, how would he, Stirling, manage? Nobody to laugh with in the middle of a piece. Nobody to grumble with when the conductor made them play allegro teararso, as they always called it. Nobody there to hiss asides to about folk in the audience.

Horny was also lying awake, half soothed by Annie's even breathing beside him and half restless with a turmoil of thoughts. Stirling was lucky, thought Horny. Life was there for him to live, and laugh about. No guilt, no sense of loss as years slid away, no edge of desperation as darkness encroached and talent shrivelled. He himself had always realised that music meant something to him which he'd never talked about, some craving for an act of creation.

He smiled in the darkness. He could just hear what Stirling would say if he could eavesdrop on thoughts like these.

'Bloody crap, that. Music's nobbut fun. Fun to play and fun to listen to. Or it bloody should be.'

Rehearsals for the concert had been and gone. Stirling had watched a new, white-faced shaking Horny facing old friends as musical director for the first time. He'd led the laughter at the awkward jokes Horny made, and leant hard into the music as urged by the trembling baton. He'd driven his flugel as never before.

He'd hated it. He'd hated having to try to be easy with Horny, with whom he'd never in his life had to try to be anything. He'd hated feeling something close to pity for Horny when he tried to explain what he wanted from the music, and couldn't find the words. He detested the spotty, snobby student who sat at his side as solo horn and showed off his technique.

'Bloody technique,' muttered Stirling under his breath. 'Yon lad'll never 'ave the deep, lovely sound that comes wi' good, 'appy livin'. He 'asn't a clue how to start to live.'

And now he was sitting in his place, concert-dressed, Snobbo next to him, waiting for Horny to appear at the side of the stage, invisible to the audience, and start them off. His heart was thumping uncomfortably, and it wasn't in march time.

'Oh, bloody ell,' he groaned. 'Bit more of this upset an I'll give up meself.'

Out of his eye-corner he saw the solo cornet waving his instrument to tell them to start, and they were off. He lost his place in his part when he saw Horny in a new white jacket looking sleek and slim (I'll bet 'e 'asn't bloody eaten this week, he thought) walking with his head high to the conductor's rostrum. Horny turned to face the audience, bowed as the band's signature piece drew to its end, then turned back to his players.

'Right, lads. Let's show the buggers,' he said.

As the last notes of the last piece crashed unevenly into each other the audience clapped, cheered and whistled as they usually did, more for pleasure in their own noise than in genuine appreciation. Horny bowed to the audience, waved the players to their feet and turned and bowed again. As he faced back to the band he leaned over the conductor's stand.

'Stir,' he said.

'Aye,' answered Stirling.

'I'm not saying I'm not glad I've done it, because I am, but thank God it's over. Get us a drink in, will you?'

They talked about it later.

'I've got to do new things every now and again,' Horny said. 'How can I find out what's inside unless I push the door open?'

'Me, I like the old, familiar, comfortable places,' said Stirling, fluent with relief and ale. 'So I know I can go in in the dark and be able to find me way.'

'Yes, but don't you ever wonder whether you mightn't find yourself in a palace, if you went through a new door,' Horny argued, 'with fountains, and sunshine, and twenty five gorgeous girls all watching the door just to see you come through?'

'Was that what we looked like to you from t'bloody middle?' asked Stirling. 'I thought you'd gone a bit funny, but seein' Tommy, Reg and me as full of Eastern Promise! Bloody 'ell, frightening that.'

'Any road, I tried it, and I'm not sorry I did. I know now I'd rather be sitting blowing. And to be honest, I'd rather have a room with Annie in than a harem.'

And later,

'You've heard 'em say, about climbing Everest, I just had to do it because it were there? Well, I suppose ...'

'Aye, but just because you see them mountaineers on telly you don't rush out and strap croutons on thi feet.'

And even later,

'Tha certainly brought a new insight into us playing.'

Pause, with Horny expectant as Stirling took a long drink.

'Aye, it were a right good change to play *Westminster Waltz* four in a bar.'

And later still,

'Nay, lad, I wouldn't say tha were bad. But the best bit about thi conducting were the way thi leant over the music stand, and wi' thi arse end pushing up the tail of yon white jacket and thi arms flappin' as well, tha looked just like a duck.'

Horny began to smile after a moment. 'I've laughed at that myself with other conductors. Did I really look like one of them wallies?'

'Put it this way,' said Stirling, consideringly. 'For a while I thought you bloody were one of them. I'm right glad you've come back to being one of us. I mean not one of the bosses. Only a player, like.'

Pontin's at Prestatyn

'Hey, our lass. D'you fancy a trip to t'sea-side?'

'What do you mean?' Dolores asked suspiciously.

T'band's decided to go in for bloody Pontin's contest at Prestatyn. End of October.'

'So it'd be there and back in a day, eh?'

'No. Some on us, like Bernard, think t'band'd play better if we stayed one night. And we need all t'help we can get wi' us test piece.'

Silence.

'Chalet accommodation.'

Silence.

'Annie can't go. One of 'er teacher mates is getting' wed.'

Silence.

'Reg's wife can't go either. She says that Reg's got to stop at 'ome Friday neet as well. Some do on.'

Silence.

'Can't mek your mind up, that it? Tempted but ... I can understand. Bloody cold in them chalets at beginning of winter. Electricity's extra. Costs a fortune. Noisy an' all – lads comin' away from t'pub a bit cheerful like.'

'How do you know?' Dolores asked sharply.

'I've been once before, remember, just to listen. And you know what young lads can be like.'

'They get no better as they get older, some of them.'

'So it's no, is it? I can't tempt you to join in wi' a bit of early winter fun?'

'Thank, Stir, but no. I'll go to our Maggie's.'

So a liberated Stirling and Horny, together with a mostly liberated band – even Lil had decided that she'd prefer to make a day of it at Harvey Nick's in Leeds – set off in a bus after work on Friday.

Two and a half hours and several crates later they arrived at a line of lights in the middle of what seemed to be a dark waste. 'Pontin's' was written over a door in the middle of the lights.

'Well, lads,' said Reg. 'We might as well go in now we're here.'

Stirling and Horny were allocated their chalet by a terrifyingly glamorous young female who handed Horny a map; she said 'We're here,' rapidly circled a spot then circled their chalet.

'Number 3993?' Horny said in a wondering voice.

'Number 393,' she told him crisply. 'Buy your electricity cards over there.'

It had almost stopped raining but was deep night when Horny and Stirling reached their chalet.

'Put the light on, Stir,' said Horny.

' 'Ow? Bloody switch dun't work.'

'Oh, aye. Electricity tokens. Where do we put them?'

'I could tell thi,' growled Stirling. 'We should have brought a bloody torch.'

They conducted a finger-tip search of the chalet.

'Hurry up, or t'bar in t'Queen Vic'll be bloody shut.'

After a few desperate minutes they gave up, leaned out of their door and shouted to a passer-by who instructed them, then they lit the lights, dumped their bags and jogged towards the pub at the front of the complex.

On the way they met Bernard, staggering under the weight of a uniform bag.

'Hurry up, Bernard. Come on, let's find your new 'ome, switch on thi lights and then buy thee a drink,' panted Stirling.

'No, no. An early night for me. I shall study the score once more, phone Lil then make myself a cocoa. I've brought some cocoa powder and milk …'

'Nay, everybody'll be in the bar,' said Horny, taking his bag. 'Folk from all the big bands as well as us third and fourth sectioned lot. Come and get talent spotted.'

'Just one, then, perhaps …'

The air was rocking around the building.

As they opened the door, 'I swear I can see the noise,' said Horny. 'Maybe when it's overwhelmed one sense it knocks over the others. Like your surfing waves, Stirling. I can fair taste this din.'

'Shut up talkin' fancy rubbish and I'll get thee summat tha can really bloody taste,' said Stirling. 'What's for thee, Bernard?'

'I might just venture to try a vodka and orange juice. I've heard it's quite refreshing. Thank you, Stirling.'

Drinks in hand, the three of them stood and looked round. It seemed that all the bandsmen in the country were there.

'How many do you reckon are here?' Horny asked Bernard.

'Well, let's see, now.' Both Stirling and Horny recognised the teacher's voice and groaned silently. 'Five sections with at least twenty bands in each section...?'

He waited expectantly.

'Right, Bernard,' said Stirling. 'Times table never went up that bloody high, but w' bandsmen and followers there must be thousands here. An' all in t'bloody bar, like I said.'

'Hey, Stir, see that girl?' asked Horny.

'What? It's like bein' in a sweet shop when I were a kid, there's too bloody many to look at. There's one bit of Edinburgh Rock,' nodding his head towards a thin, pastel-coloured girl. 'She's forgot to put 'er blouse on.'

'And there's a lass behind you, Stir, dressed like a bag of humbugs. Without wrappers. There's a shiny black and white striped bit of material just about covering her great big chest. She's got silver bobbles everywhere you can see, high heels ... Oh, I'm glad I've got Annie.'

'And that Annie's not 'ere, lad, eh?'

Bernard had sipped his drink and was beginning to make 'I must go' movements.

'Well, gentlemen,' he began, 'I ... err ...'

'No, not yet. See, there's whatsisname, our old baritone player. The lad we took to Amsterdam – you remember, Horny?'

As Bernard turned to shake hands and exchange greetings with whatsisname, Stirling said to Horny, "Ave you seen the humbugs? She's a bloody lass and a half and no mistake. She's man-handling yon tall lad 'oo's standing behind 'er. They either know each other very well or they're bloody soon goin' to.'

'We're not used to the high life in Harden Moss,' said Horny. 'Wild ways like those! And both bandsmen too, I'll bet.'

Bernard had turned back to them to say goodbye again.

'Why has the band never come here before, Bernard?' Horny went on. 'It's like the Rockies or The Great Wall of China. I'd hate to have died and not seen this place. On second thoughts, I don't really care about the Rockies and The Great Wall of China, but Pontin's of Prestatyn, now.'

Bernard finally escaped. Horny and Stirling shook hands with more old friends than they could have believed they had as they eased their way out of the bar. Trekking back through the chalet maze to their own new home they wondered to each other about women.

' 'Ow come one lass'll be wearing an anorak, track suit bottoms and trainers, standing next to another 'oo's in a bloody scrap of material as wouldn't mek me grandma a milk jug cover?'

'Men don't, do we? We all look nearly the same, even before we put our uniforms on.'

'Talking of uniforms, we'd better bloody 'ang 'em up. 'Ere's us luxury apartment.'

Two and a half minutes later,

'Night, then.'

'Night.'

It was a relaxing nine fifteen the next morning when Stirling opened the door of their chalet, shivered as the freezing wind hit him then stiffened and called urgently to Horny.

' 'Ere. Look.' He pointed.

On the far side of the quadrangle of grass which brought light and air to this part of the estate of chalets a girl was striding. She was still wearing the humbug outfit, shoulders still bare, silver baubles still glinting around the top of her black trousers, heels still high.

'Do you guess that she and that tall lad have confirmed their acquaintance? said Horny. 'Hey, what a picture.'

As the humbugs clipped rapidly east along an upper walkway a bandsman in full contest rig and carrying his instrument was walking west immediately below her.

'I reckon,' said Horny, 'that if we'd taken a photo of that, the picture could've summed up Pontin's weekend of contesting, Stir. She's obviously won one contest, the lad underneath is on his way to another.

'Isn't this place brilliant?'

Rehearsal time. Bernard had pulled friendship strings and arranged for the band to have use of Northop's famous bandroom.

'As you know, we're playing at number eleven, an excellent draw,' Bernard said comfortably as he moved around the breakfast cafeteria from table to table of his bandsmen, 'so we can rehearse at our ease and get back with no panic.'

Bernard had reached the cornets' table with his message when Widget stood and interrupted him, a high note of terror rising almost visibly in his voice.

'I'm … err … I've … errr … I'm sorry, Bernard, but I've forgot me … I've left me cornet at 'ome. Just remembered.'

Bernard sat down suddenly. His face matched his hair. He was unable to speak.

The other members of the band who were still in the café gathered around.

'What's up wi' Bernard?'

'We've just lost us top man. Or us top man 'as lost us t'contest, any road,' said Tommy.

'I'm sorry,' Widget kept repeating. He was almost in tears.

'Come on, lad,' said Horny, comfortingly. 'Someone once told me to take every set-back as an opportunity.'

'Aye. A bloody opportunity to tear us solo cornet limb from limb and feed 'im to t'sharks in t'bloody sea just over there,' said Stirling less comfortingly.

Reg took over.

'I'll take t'lad and go to instrument stands and see if we can borrow a trumpet. Right, Bernard? You get the rest of us into the coach.

Come on, Widget. It was an easy mistake to make in all the excitement.'

'What? An easy bloody mistake?' Stirling exploded as he was shuffled away quickly by Horny. 'This is a contest. You can't use words like 'mistake' about a contest. It's life or death.'

The rehearsal went as well as could be expected with Widget not only playing a new, clean instrument but with his throat so thickened by emotion that at times he could barely squeeze out a note. His only hope of playing at all seemed to be to avoid looking across the band at Tommy and Stirling and to fix his eyes on Bernard. Bernard found the experience nerve-wracking.

'*The Land Of The Mountain And The Flood*, then, gentlemen,' said Bernard as he put down his baton at the end of the rehearsal. 'A beautiful country and I want you to have in mind its beauty as you play this glorious music. See it in your mind, and your notes will convey its splendour to those listening. And, perhaps even more importantly, to ourselves.

'I look forward to our performance eagerly.'

As the band filed into the room where the Third Section Contest was being played, Horny nudged Stirling.

'Look,' he said. 'I think I recognise them there.'

'Well, I'm buggered,' said Stirling. 'Dolores, Maggie and the little lad. 'Oo'd 'ave thought they'd make the long bloody journey from Harden Moss into Wales. I'm chuffed.' He smiled at his family as he sat down and they smiled back.

'Maggie must 'ave 'ad a row wi' Shane. Having his mam-in-law to stay for the whole weekend, 'appen. He must 'ave said, 'For God's sake, tek 'er off for the day,' and they couldn't think of owt else to do.'

But he continued smiling.

All things considered, the band played well and Bernard too was smiling as he waved them all to their feet at the end.

'We're not going to come in the prizes,' he said to Reg as they moved out of the room, 'but I'm pleased. Beauty I asked for and we reached out towards it.'

'No, Stirling,' Dolores was saying. 'We came because I like the piece and we wanted to support you. And I think little Kevin here ought to start playing soon, so I wanted him to see what it's all about,'

As he left the room, Horny was button-holed by an Ancient Bandsman who talked to him for some time.

'What were that old chap tellin' you?' Stirling asked Horny later as they settled down in the band bus for the journey home.
'I liked him. Never met him before,' said Horny.
'He were telling me that someone had told him summat Howard Snell once said. Seemingly he said he could get Formica that looked like wood and it would be perfect. It'd be smooth, regular markings, perfect. And he could get real wood, with knots and flaws and the grain showing.'
Horny said nothing for a moment.
'Aye?' asked Stirling.
'And Howard Snell said he knew which he'd choose. And the old chap said our performance were real wood. What a good do, eh?'

Anaesthetic

From the corners of his eyes he was aware of shapes. Cold white shapes, squeezing the air he was breathing, filling his nostrils. The sickly smell made him panic. He forced a sound through his stiffening lips. The noise he uttered was inhuman, but it made the shapes withdraw a hair's breadth and in the space suddenly afforded him he forced his body into movement.

'You must try to stay still,' the voice behind the mask hissed at him in a terrible travesty of kindness. 'It won't be long now.'

Aeons later Stirling shuddered his way out of the nightmare.

'For goodness' sake, Stirling,' Dolores said when he swayed into the waiting room supported by the dentist and the dental nurse. 'You're the biggest baby I've ever known. Come on. Let's get you home.'

Stirling uttered a gutteral sound.

'Don't try to talk, either. Just shut up and that means stop groaning an' all.'

The drive home was as silent as Stirling could make it. He felt that his whole body was unstitched and falling apart. When the top of his head began flapping in time with the rhythm of his heart beat he dared a gentle moan. Dolores flashed one contemptuous look and he closed his eyes and sank into as small a space as his fourteen and a half stones would allow.

Time disappeared.

'Now you stay in that bed,' Dolores ordered, 'and I don't want to see or hear anything from you until I bring you a drink. Later.' She marched, small and squarely-determined, out of the darkened bedroom, pulling the door shut behind her.

It took more courage than Stirling possessed to tell her that he planned on going to rehearsal that night, 'Not to play, like. Just bloody listen,' he said as he rehearsed his undelivered speech. He tried to sneak out of the house but the stairs betrayed him.

'Planning on going somewhere? Oh, yes, and I can't guess

where,' said Dolores with heavy sarcasm when she caught him. 'Well, I'm coming with you. I fancy getting out of the house. You might just get overcome again, and chances are there won't be no nice dentist's lass to let you lean on her. Just let me get me coat.'

The November night was clean and starry. Orion marched alongside the couple as they walked towards the bandroom. From fifty yards they could hear the deeper instruments and as they drew closer the higher sounds became audible. With one mind they stopped and leaned on the wall of the road up to the bandroom.

'I allus bloody wish I knew t'names of them stars. I only know 'im up there,' said Sitrling, pointing to Orion, 'because of that test piece. All them worlds. An' some poor bugger up there is strugglin' wi' 'is part in *Poet Unpleasant*, just like Horny is now.'

Dolores smiled. 'At least I can tell what you're saying now,' she said, 'but you'll not be able to play for a while, you know. That were a big tooth that came out.'

They could hear the river rushing full of early winter rain down the valley. A dog barked in a farm up on the moors above the village. Stirling sniffed deeply and noisily.

'By bloody 'ell. It's grand to get some decent air into me lungs. I tell thee what, Dolores. This in't a bad bloody place. Where else would tha bloody choose to live?'

Dolores shivered. 'Florida,' she said.

'Nay. 'ow many 'alf decent brass bands 'ave you 'eard from bloody America? Eh? Come on. Let's go in an' listen to an 'alf decent brass band.'

As they went in Stirling whispered, 'I reckon this is t'fust time I've ever watched one of our rehearsals. Dun't know 'ow I'll bloody cope.'

Poet and Peasant had got beyond Horny's soulful part and the music was capering merrily, or at least Bernard was trying to get his group of joiners, farmers and insurance salesmen to caper.

Horny waved a hand to the newly arrived audience.

Stirling listened and winced and suffered for five minutes then muttered to Dolores 'I've 'ad enough.'

'Was it your tooth that was giving you gyp?' she asked as they crept out of the bandroom.

'It were that bloody racket. You can't always 'ear 'ow bad it is from t'middle. Owt on telly, is there?'

'I fancy a walk. If your tooth isn't going to hurt. It's a lovely night.'

'Many a bloody year since we went walking, lass. Aye, Let's do that.'

They walked through the empty streets of terraced houses which were buttoned up tight against the cold like the walkers. Yellow light seeped through curtains and Dolores noticed colours and patterns, and spilled through glazed front doors on to family cars and Stirling noticed makes and ages. They headed in silent harmony for the brighter lights of the tiny village square. They found it pulsating with teenage acne and alcohol. Boys on bikes were leaning in groups talking prowess outside the pizza parlour.

'Fancy a good old English curry?' asked Stirling. 'Horny and me often 'ave one after rehearsal. An' I 'ad nowt for me tea tonight.'

'No, but I'll have a bag of chips,' said Dolores. 'It'll take me back to our courting days. I used to tell the girls at the mill how you used to treat me. A walk then a bag of chips, with bits if you were feeling generous.'

The pleasant medley of smells from the different take-away shops concentrated itself into the hot fizzing pungency of the chippy. They leaned against the wall as they queued and read the notices. The familiar call to the Saturday concert in the bandroom made Stirling thoughtful.

As they walked away with their bags, folded in newspaper, filled to overflowing with salty, vinegary, fat, delicious chips Stirling said, 'I were thinkin' in there, does it ever worry you, me bein' out every Saturday night? All our bloody married lives, like? I mean, we've never talked about it.'

Dolores ate four chips before she answered. 'It did, you know. Back when Maggie was little. It used to seem unfair.'

Stirling wolfed his last chips, screwed the bag up and threw it towards a rubbish bin. It missed. He was walking on when Dolores said 'Hey'. He turned back, stooped, picked up the greasy paper and put it in the bin.

'You do that when I tell you. Would you have given up the band?'

Stirling thought as they turned down to walk beside the river. Finally he said, 'That's bloody hard, that. Don't know if I can answer it. Why did you never ask me?'

'I suppose I saw it made you content. And if a man's content then it makes life easier, somehow. Here. D'you want to finish my chips?'

'Aye. Ta. Mebbee I should've thought about you a bit more.'

'Why? We're here, aren't we, walking along together, talking, even though it's for the first time in however many years. And don't think I haven't had some fun out of the band.' Stirling winced. 'That your tooth?'

'No. I were remembering that Harvest bloody Festival. An' you. Doin' the strip ...'

'Right!' she interrupted.

After a moment she laughed, and Stirling joined in without knowing why they were laughing.

'It did me,' she began then collapsed into laughter again. They leaned against a wall, whooping and hiccuping with shouts of laughter. 'It did me good. It got us some right grand cuts of meat from Dyson's,' she managed. 'And yon snooty wench at the Post Office blushed every time she saw me for months after. It were worth it for that.'

'And you were big enough to tek it ... ' long deliberate pause '... as I remember,' said Stirling.

They pulled themselves together and turned for home.

As Dolores fitted her key into the lock Stirling said, 'Hey, lass, tha's missed that programme you go on about every week.'

'Never mind,' said Dolores. 'Annie'll tell me all about it. She's better than the telly, is Annie. Does Horny know what a good actress she is?'

' 'E certainly does. Says that there's times when he dun't know 'oo 'e'll be findin' when 'e gets 'ome. New woman every night.'

'Just like his young days,' they said together, and laughed again.

Later, as they were going to bed, Dolores said to Stirling, 'I've right enjoyed tonight. It's been nice talkin'. And it were lovely bein' tekken out for a fish supper. Just like my young days.'

'Well don't bloody count on it 'appenin' again.' said Stirling. 'Must 'ave been the effects of that bloody anaesthetic.'

Christmas

'Nay, love,' Stirling had said to Dolores in the early years of marriage. 'I'll only have toneet and tomorrow neet out, then mebbee an hour or two on Christmas Day. You've got no call to feel 'ard done by. And you'll come to our concert, won't you?'

In the slightly later years of marriage his response was on the lines of 'Bloody 'ell. It can't tek two people to hang balls on an imitation bloody tree. And our Maggie'll be 'appy enough on Christmas morning wi'out me. I should be back for me Christmas dinner. I'll be that hungry.'

As the marriage settled the Harden Moss Band's Christmas routine also settled and hardened. Most nights in the week before Christmas the band would play in the village's pubs, and those of surrounding villages with no bands of their own, accruing band funds. One night was always donated to the big Christmas concert in the band room which the bandsmen believed that their women and children enjoyed. Christmas Eve was celebrated magnificently with the band playing carols in the village square at midnight, and on the day itself the band split into two or occasionally three (when the women for some reason lost their grip on even more of the men than usual) and played along the streets for all the unfortunate people tangled up in the festivities.

Dolores fell asleep in the small hours of Christmas morning with the gentlest of carols, *Silent Night*, shimmering in the frosty air across the roofs and houses, hearing above the other instruments the soaring of Stirling's flugel. She woke as he climbed into bed beside her and murmured sleepily 'That sounded nice.'

Stirling turned on his side towards her. 'Eh, lass, tha'rt awake. 'Appy Christmas.'

In his house high above the valley Bernard had been listening to the band playing their celebration of Christmas. His bedroom window was wide open and he had heard the carols very faintly, sounding like the harmony of the spheres, he thought, and smiled at the fancy. Tears were sliding down his cheeks. It felt for him like a kind of goodbye. It was the first year when he had not played Christmas in at midnight.

He thought about the continuity which the band represented. Without thinking about it, the present bandsmen played many of the same tunes as their grandfathers, as well as the brilliant new compositions. The band was the musical accompaniment for the same great occasions of the year: Harvest, Christmas, Whitsun. It played at the marriages of its extended family, and for their funerals. It marched through the village streets to celebrate the Harden Moss Feast Days.

Its members welcomed the young players, who had learnt their trade in the junior band he had started, with caustic tolerance, smacking arrogant heads, teaching self-discipline, praising judiciously. It was a grumbling, irritating, hard-working unit, and together the bandsmen and their conductor made glorious, heart-shaking music.

He lay awake for a long time thinking about the people in the band, the comical, fractious, weak, generous, lazy, pompous, nervous individuals who blew together, knowing that the friends on either side of them realised their strengths and weaknesses and would always, unthinkingly, be ready in support.

Finally, full of love, he fell asleep.

Christmas Day dawned cold and bright.

'Bloody mad we must be' said Stirling to Horny as he came out of his front door and gently pulled it closed behind him. 'Annie asleep, is she? She's got some bloody sense. Come on then, let's mek our usual dignified way up to t'bandroom. We're no more bloody late than normal.'

The men in their uniforms stamping their feet and blowing on their hands cheered Horny and Stirling.

'Nay, surely we're never the last. Anyroad, let's get going,' said Horny. 'Splitting up, are we? Takes me back to school days, this. I bags Stir, Tommy, Reg, Ticker and Widget. Oh, and Tim, you come along with us. We'll go round by the new estate, down Battye Street and meet the rest of the band in the square, then we can work out which pubs we're going to target.

'Right, lads. Let's march and get some feeling back into us fingers. I'll never be able to play like this. And me valves are going to freeze any second. They're at that frightening, light-as-air stage, you know.'

They set up their first pitch, a silent, car-less cross roads at the beginning of the new houses and started with *Hail Smiling Morn*, as tradition dictated. Women opened their kitchen doors to listen. Children ran down paths, zooming aeroplanes, crawled out with car transporters or Ferraris or marched towards the group of players banging their own drums.

'Yon littl'un keeps better bloody time than young Tim,' said Stirling as they turned to *Christians Awake*. 'Mebbee we could offer him a mince pie to come round wi' us.'

Tricia, Tommy's daughter, and Josie, Widget's wife, had the collecting boxes. They went from house to house and collected smiles and thanks as much as money.

'They're comers-in. They've never had a band play to them before,' said Tricia to her dad. 'They think it's wonderful. Southerners.'

'Hey up, look at that!' said Horny to Stirling with a depth of Christmas feeling in his voice. 'She's a wonderful woman is our Lil. Who else would dare to walk through the streets wearing a Mother Christmas stripper's outfit. Well, I can imagine her stripping, anyroad.'

Stirling turned and saw the figure in clinging red velvet, white fur edging the hood and the front fastening which undulated violently over Lil's curves. She wore a very short tight skirt in the same velvet and thigh-high, high-heeled Prince Charming boots. She was teetering along, clinging to Bernard's arm.

Bernard watched the group of bandsmen. Every head swivelled as one and all eyes focused on Lil, widening to take in her full glory. Mechanically they continued playing *Jingle Bells*, with Widget's festive obligato accompaniment which had become more extraordinary every year. Eyes were still wide with wonder as they turned to *Hark the Herald*.

'Bloody 'ell,' said Stirling with deep feeling. 'I bet she's made Bernard's Christmas already.'

Bernard was still in the same reflective mood which had occupied him during the early hours. He and Lil had left their car, which Lil's high heels made obligatory, and walked towards the bright brass notes which got clearer and stronger in the traffic-less air as they tracked the sound through silent streets. He saw the group in the distance. Bright green uniforms gleaming with gold braid. Bright instruments flashing pure gold in the sun. Bright faces ruddy with cold and happiness. Red, green and gold. They were playing carols which still, it seemed to Bernard, celebrated Christmas more joyfully than too much food and television.

'Well, by bloody 'ell if it isn't our Dolores.' Stirling missed a *Glory to the Newborn King* as he watched Dolores marching squarely towards them. 'What d'you reckon I've done, Horny?'

' 'Ello, love. Nice to see you. Nowt wrong, is there?'

'I thought I'd come and collect for you. I'm not cooking dinner. Have you forgotten that we're going to Maggie's? What in the world does Lil think she looks like?'

Lil and Dolores took the collecting boxes and set off up the street to the next group of houses. Stirling and Bernard watched. Dolores wore a serviceable brown coat and sensible shoes. Lil was a pantomime dame dressed as Mother Christmas. In her high heels she was well over a foot taller than Dolores. She undulated as she walked, partly because of the shoes. Dolores stomped steadily. Bernard and Stirling caught each other's eye and smiled. Bloody 'ell, 'e's human, thought Stirling.

Bernard was also thinking. Why do women want to be so different from one another? he wondered. Look at Lil beside Dolores. Yet Tommy and Widget and Reg and Ticker and Stirling and Horny might be mistaken for one another at a quick glance. Tim will grow to fit. I know it's partly the uniform, but they have the same sort of hair, the same broad build, even their faces are alike. And they are standing in a close-knit group which represents the true nature of their interest. They belong and like it. The women are different and like it. Perhaps women focus on their own small family and men wish to share a group life with each other.

I've never truly belonged, he thought. I've always wanted to but never quite managed it. Lil was in charge of the family and I represented an acquiescent voice and financial support. It was the same with the band. As musical director I've always been an outsider. Looked up to, perhaps, deferred to on the surface but powerless in the group.

Perhaps half belonging isn't too bad, he thought.

As the pale sun swung toward the keystone of its shallow arch they moved into the older streets near the village centre, Batty Street, Hinchliffe Street and Marsden Street. The residents here knew the pattern of the day and mince pies and drinks were laid on for the players in several of the houses. Sounds mellowed and blurred a little as the players did.

Annie came out of her house as they approached. She put her arms round Horny and hugged him. 'I love Christmas,' she said. 'Thank you for my stocking.'

'You're a bloody traitor to the cause,' said Stirling bitterly to Horny. 'Now Dolores'll ask Annie what you give 'er. And what did you bloody give 'er?'

'You heard,' said Horny. 'A stocking.'

'Very bloody clever. Only one? In case she lost one of 'er legs, were it?'

'I did stuff a few things in.'

'Like bloody what? Ashamed of what you put in are you? This must be what a bloody dentist feels like.' He unconsciously rubbed his cheek.

'A gold chain, hidden inside a packet of Smarties. A nice tortoiseshell comb to stick in 'her hair when she puts it up. Just a few things like that. Nowt amazing. What did you give Dolores?'

There was silence from Stirling.

'Go on.'

'I don't need to tell you.'

'Who's ashamed now?'

'A very, very, really bloody nice bucket. No bloody need to laugh like that. She wanted a bucket. And a window cleaning sponge and squeegee. Took some finding, I can tell you. Bloody 'ell, I spent hours in B&Q. Oh, and a step ladder. A folding one. Red. I offered 'er a box of chocolates and she said not to bother. So I didn't.'

'Come on,' said Widget to the group. 'Last pub before we split and go home. Let's make it good. *Angels from the Realms* to start, then.'

They stood and played and the noise in the pub gradually gave up the battle. The women in the bar started singing, their voices tiny in comparison with the voices of the cornet, horn, euphonium, trombone and bass, and as they played *Oh Come All Ye Faithful* the players could see, in the half darkness of the bar, that everyone's mouth was keeping time. The collecting boxes had been filled and emptied and filled again. Band funds would be able to provide Tim with new timps next year.

'Merry Christmas,' they called to each other as they separated to walk to their homes. 'It's not been as painful as we thought. It'll be lovely to get warm though.'

Bernard opened the car door for Lil. 'I can't wait to get these boots off,' she said.

'I hope you enjoyed your morning, my dear,' said Bernard. 'You look absolutely wonderful, but you know that. Thank you for coming.'

'Well,' said Horny to Dolores as he and Annie paused at their door to say goodbye, 'you'll be glad to get home so you can play with your Christmas presents, I expect.'

'Bastard,' said Stirling to Horny.

Hair

It was early January. The bandroom was full for the Saurday evening concert. Horny and Stirling, in their seats as solo horn and flugelhorn, had a good view of the audience.

'Hey,' hissed Horny to Stirling. 'What's happened to thy lass's head?'

Bernard had perfected his reproachful look after long years of standing conducting directly in front of Horny and Stirling. He used it.

As the concert progressed Stirling tried to get glimpses of his wife as she sat in her usual place. Her back was to him and he could only see the top of an exotically curled and colourful creation which he assumed must belong to her because of where it was.

During Bernard's introduction of the next item Horny returned to the subject. 'Were you at home for tea?' he asked. 'Did you sit opposite that and not notice it?'

Bernard's reproach intensified.

As he blew his accompaniment to Widget's solo *Believe Me If All Those Endearing Young Charms* Stirling thought about the earlier part of the evening. Tea. What had they had? There had been something unusual. Oh aye. She'd said she hadn't had time to cook so they had egg and chips. Had she explained why she hadn't time to cook? The answer exploded in his head. With the joy of a crossword solver working out the last clue he remembered. She'd been to the hairdresser's. He supposed he ought to have looked at the result, on her head. But he'd been reading the sports page of the Examiner at the time.

At the interval Stirling took his second pint to Dolores' table.

He sat down and looked at her.

'Bloody 'ell,' he said. It was as though the egg and chips had been served with hollandaise sauce and Chablis. Her face looked the same as usual but her hair flounced and pirouetted like a horse dancer at a circus. It was bronze and polished, so she looked as if she was wearing the piled-up metallic hair of a statue of an eighteenth century French courtesan.

Or old tart, as Stirling put it to himself.

' 'Ow much did that bloody cost you?' he breathed.

'What? Oh, you mean my hair. Nothing. It were free. That nice Giovanni did it, you know, him who's taken that little hut out on Moor Road.' She patted the outworks gingerly. 'Like it, do you?'

Before Stirling could speak Bernard called him back on to the stage. He had only time to swallow his pint and go, with a livid backward glance at Dolores.

'Did you ...' began Horny.

'Shut thi bloody face,' growled Stirling. 'Some bloody Eytie givin' hairdoes away free.'

'Makes you wonder why,' said Horny as they launched into *Bells Across The Meadow*.

Stirling broke with the tradition of a life-time and went straight home that night. He caught Dolores unawares, examining every angle of her hair with the aid of a hand mirror and the mirror over the mantlepiece.

'What's that nice bloody Giovanni's game?' Stirling shouted as he swung the door shut behind him.

Dolores jumped at the crash and her hair jumped rigidly with her.

'Hello, Stirling. You're back early. Not a bad concert, I thought.'

'Never mind bloody concert. Tell us about this hairdresser.'

'He's very nice. Lovely foreign accent, and lovely hands and ...'

'I'll bloody bet 'e's got lovely bloody 'ands. What I want to know is what did 'e do wi' them?'

'Styled my hair. He said it were a criminal shame what I'd had done to my hair before.'

'There's a bloody crime somewhere, I'm damn sure of that. 'Ow come 'e give you that thing on yer 'ead free?'

'Well, him and me chatted like you do, when you're having your hair done ...'

'No bloody barber chats wi' me,' Stirling growled.

'... and when he brought up the subject of the band, and I said

you played, he seemed right excited, and said my hairdo were free ...'
She hesitated, 'if ...'

'It's that 'if' I don't like. If bloody what?'

'If I promised to mention him to you, and ask if he might be able to sit in on a rehearsal. I didn't think that'd be a problem. It's not, is it?'

Time had fitted another length of pipe to the decaying plumbing system which was Stirling's life when Dolores said to him, over his favourite tea of home-made meat and potato pie with onion gravy, carrots and cabbage, 'Thought I'd bring that Giovanni to the bandroom tonight.'

It always took a moment or two for thoughts to flow through the heavily scaled deposits within Stirling's intellectual pipework. With the extra blockage of meat and potato pie and the sports page the flow became a trickle.

At last he said 'Oh, aye. Oo's 'e when 'e's at 'ome?'

'The hairdresser who styled my hair last week. Him from the hut on Moor Road.'

Stirling came to life. ' 'Im what took bloody advantage of you?'

'What d'you mean?'

' 'Im what sent you out wi' that curly 'elmet on your 'ead. You looked like a poofing soldier in Jason and the bloody Argonauts.'

'Well ... Him. There won't be a problem if we turn up, will there?'

Bernard and the band were working on the test piece they were going to take for its first outing to Dewsbury before sweeping up all the prizes at Holmfirth in May.

'Good evening, gentlemen.' Bernard always tried to begin a rehearsal on an optimistic note. 'I was really quite pleased with the first movement last week. I thought we created the '*Country House*' atmosphere with some nobility.'

The band rumbled coarse agreement.

'And I'm sure we won't find the second section, '*Gardens*', which we haven't looked at yet, any problem. After all, we're noted for our slow playing. It's 'Funfair' which is likely to be a bit of an up-and-downer for us. So let's take a run at it. Gentlemen, the *Alton Towers Suite*, third movement, please.'

After half an hour spent screaming around the rides, which should, by the sound of them, have been shut down seasons ago, Bernard became aware that he'd lost the band's attention. He turned and saw Stirling's wife standing diffidently at the back of the bandroom, with a man. He received an impression of a small, flamboyant person, rather like a brightly-decorated plaster statuette from a cheap gift shop on the Italian Riviera, before he turned back.

'Now then, can we have just the cornets at Letter D and let's use our instruments to make the girls scream in excitement. Ready?'

At the break Stirling and Horny stayed in their places and watched the little man being courteously greeted by Bernard. They heard drifts of conversation.

'I'm Bernard and as Musical Director of Harden Moss Band I'm very pleased to welcome any visitor to our bandroom. I hope you enjoyed the rehearsal.'

'Eet was - 'ow you say - magnifico,' the newcomer gushed. 'I, Giovanni Batista, love ze brassabandamusica. So ... so macho.'

Stirling and Horny looked down from the stage on an anxiously-smiling brown face under luxuriant shiny wavy black locks. Each of them unconsciously ran a hand over his own disappearing hair.

'Don't know why you were so worried about Dolores being taken advantage of by yon lad,' said Horny. 'Doesn't look to me like he could take advantage of a free sausage on a stick.'

'I'm not bloody sure,' said Stirling. 'I reckon 'e'd enjoy a sausage on a stick.'

They listened again. 'Yes, by all means. Bring your instrument along to our next rehearsal and we'll give you an audition.'

'What?' exploded Stirling in a subterranean sort of way. 'Yon diddyman's bein' tried out for t'band? Niver. Just picture 'im on t'bloody stage beside the likes of us an' Tommy an' Reg. Men, like.'

'Be fair, Stir,' said Horny. 'He might be just what the back row needs.'

'Aye. There's one or two in t'bloody back row need summat to wake 'em up, right enough,' said Stirling. 'And then we could always use 'im for our mascot. If we could get a little enough jacket.'

Just then Giovanni vaulted lightly on to the stage and with a flashing smile at Horny and Stirling picked up Widget's cornet, blew into it and began to play, looking at the top man's part as he did so.

For the first time since starting work on the movement Stirling could follow a thread of melody. The sound swooped and plunged and Stirling was twisting and spinning with it so that, as the sound dropped, he found himself saying 'D'you know, Horny, that made me realise why I 'ate fairground rides - mek me that bloody dizzy ... And hey, I niver knew an Eytie could mek a proper bloody noise on a trumpet.'

The other members of the band came back to their places, smiling appreciatively. Giovanni's teeth gleamed again as he handed back the cornet. 'Mille thank-yous,' he said.

'So you'll come for a full rehearsal then. Next Thursday, if that's all right with you. And you do have your own instrument?' enquired Bernard

'Si, si. Now I take the lovely Dolores 'ome. Arrivaderci,' and the little man's crimson velvet loon pants danced him towards the bandroom door.

Over their beer in the pub later that evening Horny gave Stirling wise advice about women.

'First, never give them the upper hand by letting on that th'art jealous,' he said. 'Second, never be jealous until tha've seen the other bloke, with thy lass an' all. And third, always remember that most men'd rather have a good evening with their mates than get involved with a woman. Even somebody else's.'

'Easy to be seen that you've never been bloody wed, and that you an' Annie don't lead a normal life,' said Stirling. 'It'll 'ave done our Dolores a power of good. The lovely Dolores, eh? Can't wait to get 'ome. Just time for me to get us another pint, and then it'll be thy round after ...'

Giovanni in the Band

Giovanni's first rehearsal had just ended and small knots of bandsmen were discussing him

'No, lad. I don't agree,' said Horny. 'He plays well, he's pleasant enough.'

'Aye, that's just it. Tha's hit t'bloody nail. 'E's that pleasant 'e's not real.'

'Well, he's not. He's from Italy, isn't he?'

Stirling's face took on an even uglier look than normal. 'But is 'e?'

'What?'

'Is 'e an Eytie? That fancy way 'e talks, all 'Bellisima' and bloody whatnot. Might go down all right in 'is 'ut on t'Moor Road, wi' the likes of t'women, but I wouldn't mind bettin' 'e goes 'ome at night on t' buz!'

'Are you feeling all right? What do you mean? What's a buzz, if a wasp isn't wearing it?'

'A bus from Lancashire, you stupid bugger. Where were you educated? No, I didn't mean that. I know bloody well. And I've always said Bernard has a lot to answer for. Hey up, 'e's here. Nah, then, Giovanni, sit down and wrap thi hands round yon pint. And tell us about where tha learnt to play like that. Lovely bloody sound. Reminded me a bit of Harry Mortimer. And Phil McCann.'

The small man swung a third chair out from under the table, sat, crossed his legs and lifted his glass with both hands. He took a long drink and lowered the level of the beer just perceptibly.

Stirling watched with astonishment. 'Yon lad sips 'is beer,' he whispered to Horny. 'Must be from Lancashire.'

'You aska where I learn to play si bene?' Giovanni began, putting down his glass carefully. 'My papa, ee was maestro for a band een Naples where we leev. Ver', ver' beautiful place. And I go weeth my papa to leesten and I love zee music so much my papa geev me trumpeto to try weeth, and so I play. Eet was always easy for me.'

'When did you come up 'ere, lad? God's own country, like.'

'My papa bring us to Eengland, when he come to work weeth hees brother een feesh and cheep shop. I no like. Eet smell bad. I lika ze beautiful scents. And beautiful musico. Like the music we play tonight. So I leave and join salon, and train, but I mees ze music.'

Two more pints were plonked on the table and Reg joined the group. 'That un's for thee, lad. Tha played a treat. Pity tha're not a bass player.'

Tim, short for Timpanist, the band's sad, mad percussionist, was clutching his glass of lemonade and looking as though he wanted to join the group.

Horny slapped his palm on the spare chair at the table.

'Come on, then, Tim, lad. Park thi arse here. This isn't a real musician, Giovanni. He plays the instruments of war, as I once heard a conductor call 'em. We're hearing the tale of how Giovanni here started playing, young'un. Listen, and you might make a real bandsman yet.'

The evening wore on. Giovanni's face took on a glossier look, his mouth wavered when he tried to talk and he giggled as he sipped yet another drink, this time a yellowish confection which looked as though it ought to have had whipped cream on top. By now he was choosing his own drinks, after the hard men of the band had realised the danger that their gift-beer might be unsupped. His Italian accent was wavering too, and slipping ever closer to the Lancashire border.

Finally Horny asked the question. 'Come on, Gio, lad. You've never been to Italy, have you?'

Giovanni giggled his answer.

'Still bloody amazin', if 'e can play like that, comin' from Lancashire.'

' 'Ow come you look foreign?' Reg asked simply.

Giovanni giggled some more. Helplessly.

'My papa - sorry -' he collapsed in tears of laughter. ' Me dad went to Italy when he joined the army, like, and he really loved the dark, sexy Italian girls. So when he came home he looked for a Lancashire girl who was small and dark and married her. She turned out a real tartar and me dad buggered off, with another little dark lass.'

'D'you want another of them things in the glass?' interrupted Horny, getting up heavily. 'Another weak lemonade for you, Tim?'

A long hour later the bar lights were dim and yellowed, like the tired eyes of the last few men still sitting and talking. Finally Stirling and Horny admitted defeat and got up to leave.

'Nah, Gio, lad, you'll find your way home easy if you sets off with the wall of pub on your right - no - left, tha's right.'

'No, bloody left, tha daft bugger.'

'Tha's what I said, didn't I?'

'Anyroad, Tim might not be a bloody musician, but at least 'e lives 'ere. So 'e should be able to 'elp thi, an' we'll see thi on Sat'day neet, for t'concert, if tha gets 'ome, that is.'

As they walked along the silent midnight streets, Stirling and Horny amused themselves with making up an ideal concert programme to feature Giovanni.

' 'E could play that well-loved cornet solo *Fairies of the Water*,' Horny began.

'Aye, an' we could follow that wi' *Puff the Magic Dragon*'.

'No, no. We want *Queen's Bohemian Rhapsody* next,' insisted Horny.

'A selection from t' *Gay* bloody *Nineties*?'

'With *The Lonely Ballerina* to follow.'

'I've always liked 'Enry Mancini's *Pink Poofter*,' said Stirling, and the pair of them sang 'Bedum, bedum, bedumbedumbedum...' improvising a double cross-over dance step at the same time.

'We could play a trio, you, me and 'im: *The Good, the Bad and the Ugly*.' The streets vibrated to the ululation of the theme song, harmonised by two very cheerful bandsmen. '

'Who's who, though?' asked Horny, and they found this extraordinarily funny.

'And ... we'll finish off ...' Stirling couldn't speak, 'and we'll finish t'concert ...'

'Spit it out,' said Horny, laughing in sympathy.

'And we'll finish with ... sorry ... it's just so bloody funny ... we'll play *Dance of the Sugar Plum Fairy*.' Helplessly they staggered against the nearest wall.

When they were able to walk on, Stirling said to Horny. 'Are we mekkin' assumptions 'ere? 'Ow do we know t'lad's nobbut a bloody nine bob note?'

'Young Tim fancied him, that's for sure. I've never seen Tim happy, and he only looked half miserable tonight.'

' 'Appen 'e wants to try out 'is paradiddles in private,' said Stirling. 'Eh, well. We'll see. We've got 'ome quick. See you Saturday, for t'concert.'

Bernard conducted the concert in his customary school-teacherly way, giving musical-history lessons between the pieces, which allowed the audience time to catch up on gossip, and the band time to get their breath back. Each soloist was introduced with a short biography, most of which had been familiar to the listeners since early childhood. So when Giovanni stood up from his position as bumper-up there was an unfamiliar silence in front of him as Bernard spoke.

'Ladies and gentlemen, it gives me particular pleasure to introduce a new player to you, someone who we very much hope is going to join us for the future. Giovanni Batista, a creative talent in the village, as my wife, like many of our ladies, has very delightfully shown, has chosen for his debut solo to play a classic which has been recorded by many fine players from Willie Lang to Philip McCann. Ladies and gentlemen, *Jenny Wren*.'

The sweet warbling notes flowed like clear water. Stirling concentrated on following Bernard, and rippling his accompaniment softly as background to the solo, but he snatched a quick look at Tim standing, hands folded, behind his drums. His head was bent, but Stirling could have sworn that he saw a light shining on the drum-skin, as though it was the reflection of a lamp glowing in Tim's face.

'Poor bloody sod,' he said to himself.

Giovanni gathered the applause with confidence that it was his due. His bows had a flourish which was absent from the usual soloists' stolid embarrassment. He swung round, smiling, to collect the band's generous applause.

Stirling was suddenly aware that he didn't like the man.

'If a man can cheat about where he's from,' he thought, 'when can he be trusted? Your home's part of you. No. He's not right for this place. He doesn't fit Harden Moss. I don't want him to stay.'

Goodbye, Giovanni

Stirling sat in his armchair into the early hours of the morning after the second Saturday evening concert in which Giovanni had played. He sat staring at the cold fire and thinking. He and Horny had hardly spoken as they drank their customary post-concert beers. Nothing unusual in that. But Stirling had been uncomfortable. He didn't want to discuss it with Horny, because he wasn't clear enough in his head, but he felt increasingly certain, with every week that passed, that there was something wrong about Giovanni and he didn't want him in the band. Or in Harden Moss, in fact.

Finally he gave up the effort to think, decided that he would after all have to talk to Horny who was cleverer than him and would know what to do, went to bed, hooked an arm over Dolores for comfort and went to sleep.

The next evening he found Horny in his garden shed.

'Fancy a pint?' asked Stirling, unnecessarily.

'Go on, then, tell me. What was up with thee last night?' asked Horny, ignoring the question.

'I don't know what the bloody 'ell you mean ... oh, all right. There's summat wrong wi' that incomer in the band. And it's not that I wouldn't feel safe pickin' up a penny I'd dropped wi' 'im around. Go on, Horny. You tell me. I'm bloody fast for a reason.'

' I need to get to know a bit more about him before I can give you one. I remember I said he was pleasant, but I agree, there is summat just not ... And I'm sorry for young Tim. He's going to get the stuffing knocked out of him. And he hasn't got enough stuffing to lose. D'you agree with me, about Tim, I mean?'

'Aye. Long streak of rain watter. An' he thought the sun 'ad come out, wi' yon bloody fake. Tim's a student, isn't 'e? Doesn't 'e live by hisself in a flat in one of them 'ouses our bass section owns, up by top bus stop? I don't think I've ever 'eard 'im speak. Teks it all out on t'drums.'

'Nice enough lad, but lonesome. Right, then. Now I know

what's up with thee we'll go and have a pint.'

Reg was in the pub.

'Yon bright spark, Gio whatsit were in 'ere just now. Thrilled with 'imself over t'concert. I must say that '*Jenny Wren*' piece were a treat. I 'aven't 'eard it for years. 'E were talkin' as if 'e'd be top man soon. 'Ow's that? Is young Widget leavin'?'

'Not that I know of,' said Horny. 'Nothing wrong with Widget in top chair. He's good and reliable. Nothing flashy, but sound. Was Giovanni criticising him?'

'No. Well, no, not really. It was just obvious that Gio knew 'e was a better player, that's all. Any road, there's no way band committee'd swop an old stager like young Widget for an infiltrator.'

'That's it,' Stirling suddenly said. "That Giovanni's a bloody infiltrator. 'E's infiltrated our village, and got round our lasses, wi' 'is fancy bloody 'airdoes, an' now 'e's infiltrating our band. For 'is own purposes!'

'It's not like you to be over-dramatic,' said Horny. 'What's in it for him if he does get into the band?'

'Nay, Horny. You don't expect me to know that. I just feel that we're being tekken over, and made to do things we don't really want to, just so Gio-bloody-vanni can be centre stage. Mebbe I'm wrong, eh, Reg? It's not as if I've 'ad much practice in not trusting folk.'

'Even the folk you don't like you can trust in this village,' said Horny. 'I don't like my boss, but I know just what the bastard's going to do.'

'Aye, and when 'e's goin' to do it,' added Stirling. 'Same wi' Dolores' family. D'you know, 'er mother's always saying I bloody swear! Tells me off about it. Me! Bloody 'ell!'

It was later that same evening when Horny and Stirling, on their way to buy a curry, saw sad mad Tim weaving a dangerous path from side to side of the main road through the village. Without a word they formed up on either side of him, turned him round and led him towards the throbbing heart of Harden Moss.

'Nah then, summat in your stomach is what you bloody need. What's going to lie there easiest? The fish and chips are mebbee a bit on the greasy side.'

Tim's head retched forward at the thought.

'An' the curry can be bloody lethal, especially when it gets to closing time.'

Tim lolled against the wall, held vertical by Horny's steadying hand.

'A simple old-fashioned pizza, eh, Tim?'

Tim's eyes filled with tears, and he rolled his face against the rough stone of the friendly wall which was helping Horny to hold him up.

Horny hissed at Stirling, 'You daft sod. Haven't you heard that pizzas come from the home of people called stupid names like Giovanni? Go and get him a teacake and chips. It'll be mainly teacake at this time of night any road.'

While Stirling queued Horny rolled Tim along the wall to the bus stop, propped him in the corner and sat down beside him.

'Been drinking, lad? You've not had a lot of practice, have you? It gets better as you get older. Like life, really. There's not a lot to be said for being young as I recall. Well, now I start recalling there are certain things ... but lasses aren't right special to you, are they?'

Horny looked at Tim, and put a large comforting hand on his skinny, shivering knee.

'Sorry. I reckon I hope you'll be able to like people, whatever sex. And to like people you've got to be able to trust them. And to be able to trust them, mebbee you've got to be lucky. D'you want to talk about what's happened to you tonight?'

Horny explained what had happened as he and Stirling were walking slowly and sadly home from Tim's tiny, dirty, dishevelled room where they had washed his face clean of tears, made him a cup of tea and rolled him in his grubby duvet.

'Places like that almost make me appreciate bein' wed,' said Stirling. 'Go on. Tell us.'

'Seems like it was just as I said. Giovanni Batista knocked the stuffing out of that poor lad. Was nice as pie to him, got him eating the pie out of his hand then told him he was drippy, boring and couldn't play the drums.'

'Well, we knew all that. Though we'd not 'ave told 'im,' Stirling added hastily.

'He got him all lit up with happiness, just to make himself feel powerful. He fed him disgusting drinks which he told him were sophisticated, then kicked him where the poor lad was most vulnerable, and left him to find his way back to that pig stye he calls home. What can you say about someone like that?'

'Well, one thing's for sure. 'E's no bloody Yorkshireman,' said Stirling.

Stirling had another wakeful night.

I will definitely talk it over with Horny tomorrow, Stirling decided before he finally slept. He's always got the best ideas about what to do. Aye, Horny'll know.

Dolores complained in the morning. 'I don't know what you and Horny were up to yesterday evening, but you were right restless in the middle of the night, twitching and kicking. I'm sure I'm black and blue.'

Tuesday rehearsal. Horny and Stirling saw the empty chair as soon as they entered the bandroom, late as usual.

'Excuse me, Bernard,' said Horny with excessive politeness. 'Sorry to interrupt.' Bernard looked suspicious then nervous. 'Is that new bloke coming tonight?'

'No. I was going to explain his absence when we reached a natural break,' Bernard said reprovingly. 'Apparently he has decided that Harden Moss band does not offer a lively enough platform for his talents. No doubt we all share my disappointment, and, I might say, sense of being let down. Now if we may be allowed to return to our rehearsal,' with heavy sarcasm, 'we'll go back to the beginning of the second movement. One two three ...'

'Well, what do you make of that,' Horny muttered to Stirling as they sat down. 'Seems as though he's gone. Just like that.'

Stirling said nothing and Horny looked at him more closely.

'You knew he wasn't coming to rehearsal tonight, didn't you?'

Stirling shook his head and tried to look surprised.

'You've done summat, haven't you? Why, you underhand ...' Horny tightened his lips and the next time they had a few bars' rest he hissed, 'Tell me later.'

Horny bought the first pints and waited until Stirling had taken a long drink before he said, 'Well?'

'Well what?' asked Stirling looking more innocent than Horny had seen him look since they were correctly accused, as six year olds, of taking Horny's mother's biscuits which she had left on the window sill to cool.

'What did you say to make him go? You didn't have a fight, did you?'

'What, me fight wi' yon bloody diddyman?' He unconsciously rubbed his knuckles and took another long drink. 'I just told 'im. Said we didn't want 'im in Harden Moss or in't band. More or less.'

'It's the more or less bit that's interesting. He were dead keen on playing with us. He wouldn't give it up just like that. And why didn't you ask me to go see him with you? He could have turned nasty, a mean ratty little thing like that.'

'I thought it were summat I ought to do. It were me what thought he were a baddun, so it was up to me to sort it. Bloody 'ell, am I not allowed to do owt on my own?'

He refused to explain. It was much later, when he was once again lying beside Dolores and unable to get to sleep, that he replayed his personal, private tape of the meeting with Giovanni.

Stirling had gone into the salon when the last lady had said effusive goodbyes and left but not before he had hung around the hut for half an hour, waiting.

'Fust time I've had to act like som'dy wi' summat to hide. Since I were a kid, anyroad,' he muttered as he pushed open the door without knocking. Giovanni looked round in surprise, saw him and smiled.

'You wanting a decent hair-cut?' he said.

'No. I want to talk to you,' said Stirling.

'You won't mind if I clear up. So busy, you know how it is. So popular with your ladies here.'

'I suppose it's that I've come to discuss. I want to know why. Why you've gone to so much bother to get on t'right side of t'women. Then why you've got yourself set up in t'band. You're a bloody good player, true. Better than our little band wants. You go on playing with us and Bernard'll start thinking why don't our bloody corner men come up to your standard. And we can't.'

Giovanni was laughing. 'Yes, I know I'm good. Too good. But you're not telling me I have to get worse. I could lead you all to better things.' He stopped wiping the counter top around the basin and looked straight at Stirling. 'Are you truly happy to be second or is it third rate? Well, quite probably you are.' He laughed some more.

'Just for t'moment I can't think where you've come from,' said Stirling suddenly. 'It's not as if we know many of t'folk in far off bands in Lancashire and whatnot. But I know this: somebody who can play *Jenny Wren* like you do must 'ave 'ad experience in some top outfit.'

The hut went quiet. Giovanni's hands were still.

'So where 'ave you played? If I got on to Internet and looked 'ard in Four Bars Rest would I find some band that's been disrupted by some bloody little squirt pretending to be an Eytie? We don't know your real bloody name, do we? But I bet if I put your description into t'web some clever sod would get in touch with our poor little third rate outfit. Huh?' Stirling had probably never talked as much since being in Bernard's class.

Giovanni's hands were working mechanically, repeatedly polishing the same bit of mirror.

Stirling moved towards the door and took hold of the handle.

'I'll go to Horny's 'ouse now and do just that. Then I'll put your real name about and …'

Giovanni leapt past him and shoved his shoulder against the door.

'I'm good at what I do, hair-dressing and playing cornet. That's all. Jealous people make up stories about those who do things well. Jealous people. They can't damage me or my reputation.'

Stirling waited.

'All I want to do is what I'm good at. I don't want to cause trouble. If trouble happens it's because of jealousy.'

Stirling waited.

'It so happens that I must leave this dreary, wet, mean-spirited valley. I've been invited to play on a cruise ship. Hair-dressing and playing cornet, a wonderful, well-paid combination with all the bored, wealthy widows and divorcees. Don't you envy me? But you wouldn't. You're satisfied with your plain, thick missus. Or do you secretly fancy poor Tim?'

And this was when Stirling hit him.

Dolores was full of complaints when Stirling got home from work the following evening. Giovanni had pinned a note to his salon door cancelling all future appointments, she said. Stirling put his coat on again and went back down the street on his way to the hut on the Moor Road for the second time.

The night sky had blown itself clear of clouds and a nearly full moon was competing successfully with the Harden Moss street lights when he reached Giovanni's place. It looked almost as small and wretched in the moonlight as in the light of day. Giovanni had made an attempt to give it his own particular style with brilliantly coloured posters advertising His'n'Her-Kutz and His'n'Her-Styles.

Now the chains of lights which had winked in the window night and day since Giovanni took over the place had been switched off. A piece of Giovanni Batista notepaper was sellotaped against the glass of the door. The paper had as background Giovanni's pastel-tinted face, and his name was elaborately printed as a border all round in purple on vivid yellow. A message had been hand-written on top of the face. It was addressed to all Giovanni's dear friends. It said:

Giovanni Batista is over-whelmed with sadness that his career takes him away from this so-beautiful village. His days and nights here have been full of happiness and he thanks his dear friends and hopes that someday soon they will meet again.

There was no address and no telephone number.

Stirling read and re-read the message in silence.

'Well, he's gone,' he said aloud to the night. 'And this place is well rid of 'im. And I might just get a good night's sleep.'

He turned and walked home.

War and Reconstruction

'Have you had a look at the test piece, Tommy?' Horny said conversationally as he, Tommy and Stirling sauntered towards the urgent extra rehearsal Bernard had called for the last Wednesday evening in January. 'It's not easy, not for us bands in the third section. Mind you I suppose they might have considered that point, since it's the test piece they've chosen for the third section.'

Tommy hefted his trombone case in a demonstrative way.

'Course Ah've 'ad a look. See. Fust time Ah've 'ad to tek mi instrument 'ome to practise since Ah moved up to senior band, twenty eight year ago.'

'I bet you two won't 'ave noticed bloody tempo changes for flugel, 'ave you?' complained Stirling. 'And there's me solo in t'middle of slow movement. I shall 'ave to rely on bloody conductor to count me in there. And we all know what Bernard's like under stress. Bloody terrible. Gets the shakes like a willow tree in a wind so we've no way of telling the bloody beat.'

The three, Tommy, Stirling and Horny, strolled at a leisurely andante into the pandemonium of the bandroom. Most of the players were already there, and Bernard was standing in front of the semi circle, anxiously flicking over the pages of his conductor's score while each of the men in front of him practised his own most difficult bars. Loudly and inharmoniously.

'Bloody worse than usual,' grumbled Stirling happily. 'I mek no wonder me hearing's going.'

'You should be grateful for that just now. Hey up, he's ready.'

Solo horn and flugelhorn were taken hurriedly out of their cases and Horny and Stirling blew familiarly into the mouthpieces to warm them as Bernard gave his starting pep talk.

'Gentlemen. Thank you for coming this evening. We'll tune up with *Oh God Our Help*, and, if I may make a small joke, play it well because we need all the help we can get. Ready?'

Baton raised, they were off. The sonorous sounds of the great hymn sang, held and drifted into silence as Bernard held the last note, before finally pinching it out like a candle flame.

'Now, the first movement of the test piece.'

Dissonance, discords and cacophony succeeded the harmony of the hymn. Some of the discords were deliberate, structured in to the chaos of the newly commissioned piece, *War and Reconstruction.*

After seven breathless, struggling minutes Bernard motioned the players to silence.

'We face a challenge here,' he said. 'Or perhaps I mean I face a challenge. Basses, let me hear you, starting three bars before D. Three four … '

The heavyweights of the band humphed and pumped their dark and dismal way through the first bombs of the blitz. Stirling and Horny listened to Reg and his team.

'I've always believed in peace. War's so messy,' Horny murmured to Stirling.

'Don't know why you're bloody whispering. Not with the buildings falling down around us 'eads.'

'Now we'll add the middle of the band, horns, flugel and baritones, plus trombones. From the same place, three four …'

Chaos.

Band called to order again.

'Did baritones come in three bars before D? Are you playing semibreves, horns? You're all supposed to be adding to the weight of the ordinance. Try again. '

The front row had their fingers in their ears by this time and Bernard looked as though he wished he could do the same.

A lengthy and distressing discussion about time signatures followed.

'But if you don't beat us four four, 'ow the bloody 'ell are we supposed to keep time?'

'I'm beating twelve eight for the cornets who will be the air raid when they are included and you're just going to have to follow Tim's drum beat.'

'And we bloody know where that can lead us.' Piano from Stirling.

Bernard's face was red and his white hair was standing straight up, combed by desperate fingers.

'And 'oo's going to keep t'percussion in time?' asked Tommy.

Bernard turned away.

'A break. Five minutes, that's all.'

Bernard went outside.

'Nivver known 'im go out o't bandroom in't middle of a rehearsal,' said Tommy. 'Stressed, Ah'd say.'

'Aye, but which stress are we talking about. Stress on third beat in fourth bar or fourth beat in third bar.'

Bernard came in.

'Bloody 'ell. Look at 'is face. Come on, lads. Listen. We're about to experience the uneasy calm of t'second movement.'

Bernard tapped his baton on the edge of his music stand, and his voice sounded as small and thin as his baton when he spoke. 'Let us all make an effort to capture that tense feeling of apprehension between bouts of fierce activity which the second movement asks for.'

'Are we 'appy wi' the fust movement, then?'

'Happy wouldn't be the word I'd choose, Stirling. Resigned to abandoning the ruins of the air raid, I'd say. Don't forget we're relying on your solo in this movement.'

The music lurched forwards from a fairly common starting point.

'Bloody 'ell, Ah know just what 'e means about apprehension,' Stirling muttered and blew.

Being slow, the second movement was more manageable for the bulk of the band but Stirling screeched and parpled his way through the notes of his solo, aware, without looking at him, that the lines on Bernard's face were deepening in an agony of self control as he played. The last note died and Bernard spoke.

'Apprehension, I suggested, not blind terror, Stirling. Do you remember when the head master used to call you and Horny out of my class, when you'd both been unusually objectionable, and you used to wait outside his room? That was terror. I want something more like the feeling you had before you met Dolores's mother for the first time. Remember? Try it.'

This time the notes seemed to hang in the air. Space shivered around them.

'Much better,' said Bernard, his face glowing with momentary hope. 'Now can we try it again, and this time soften the last three notes of the cadenza.'

'I tried before,' said Stirling. 'I was using Matty here as a mute.'

'Which bit of Matty were you using?' muttered Horny.

There still remained the final challenge. Reconstruction, as pictured in the last movement.

'It's all building workers,' Stirling rumbled as he fingered his way through the first page while Bernard was mentally girding his loins. 'Now if we only 'ad to play music for t'plumbers, it'd be easy.'

Bernard physically hitched his trousers and the band began to dig the foundations before the re-building proper could begin.

In a break, while Bernard was chastising Tommy and his bass trombone for a forgotten note, Horny said to Stirling, 'This is probably the most tuneless piece of music I've ever played. How much did somebody get to write it? What's it for? It was probably commissioned by people who make hearing aids.'

'Nay, I'm not sure. I can hear a sort of a plan. Inside my 'ead the shape of the music looks a bit like the plumbing diagram for t'Town Hall. Remember? Our firm did that.'

'You're not saying you like it, are you?'

'Aye. I am, Horny. I can 'ear … Bloody 'ell. Bernard can't by t'look on 'is face. Get thi 'ead down and start t'digging again.'

The last hour of rehearsal scrambled past untidily. On the stroke of ten Bernard brought his baton down, then broke for a second time with his familiar pattern of behaviour and caught up with Horny and Stirling as they were leaving the bandroom to walk down to the pub.

'Mind if I join you, err … lads?' he said, thinly. 'I'd welcome a chance to talk about the test piece.'

Bernard fitted his steps to the normal mile an hour pace of his solo horn and flugel players and the odd trio wandered down the hill.

'It's a very difficult piece for the conductor.' Bernard broached the subject without realising that his companions knew exactly what was troubling him. 'It's largely the time signatures. There are pages in this score where each bar has a different time sign.'

The others waited for the point, slowing their pace so that they didn't reach the pub before Bernard reached the gist of his worry.

'And to put it frankly, I'm not sure I can manage it.'

Horny looked at Stirling who looked back.

'Come on in and let's buy you a bloody pint, Bernard. T'job 'll look easier through the bottom of a glass. Life always bloody does.'

'And we won't let you talk about the test piece until we've all had enough.'

Two hours later Gabby, the publican, gently led the his old teacher to the door, unlocked it and put his head out, scanning the street for blue flashing lights.

'There you go, lads,' he said to Horny and Stirling. 'Take care of him. I'm terrified of Lil.'

Stirling began the walk up the long hill to Bernard's house by instructing Bernard on the scheme of construction used when Huddersfield Town Hall was first built and then when it was refurbished.

'Nowt to do wi' bloody piece, 'cept that in the last movement I can hear 'ow the underpinnings of buildings are put together. I reckon t'composer were a plumber. I'll spell it out for thee tomorrow neet. Before regular rehearsal.'

'And I think you make the band do the work for you,' Horny contributed. 'You concentrate on conducting the story line, sort of thing, and let the twiddlers faff around playing with themselves. With Tim on timps keeping their rhythm.'

'Which means that with a couple of bloody beta blockers tha should be able to get through all reet.'

* * * *

Horny and Stirling leant, pints in hand, against the wall outside The Old Court House, now a pub, and watched the audience coming down the long stairs and out of the posh doors of Huddersfield Town Hall.

'I still can't believe it,' Horny said. 'I can't believe twenty five men let you take them round the cellars and underground rooms of that place yonder, just so you could explain your theory of construction to them. But it worked, somehow. Sixth place for us was brilliant.'

'Nowt to it, Horny. Construction, or reconstruction, I suppose, is just a matter of fitting bits together in t'right bloody order.' He took a long slow drink and smacked his lips appreciatively. 'Bugger all different to music, when you think about it.'

The Learner

Stirling was looking for a shirt.

'Bloody 'ell. Where does she keep 'em? They're always in't drawer and … What the …?'

Furious feet clattered down the stairs and Stirling's furious face appeared around the door of the kitchen where Dolores was chopping onions.

'What the 'ell is a cornet I've niver seen before doing in the chest of drawers in t'spare bloody bedroom? Eh?' He bellowed the last word ferociously. 'What I want to know is 'oo's been in this 'ouse wi' 'is cornet. And a bloody poor cornet too. 'Oo?'

By the time he got to the last 'oo, his face was an inch from Dolores' face and his voice was double forte. She shook her head.

'Honestly, Stir, the older you get the dafter you are. Shut up a minute and take your face away, or I'll be tempted to stick this onion knife up your big fat nose. So it's a poor cornet, is it? What do you mean?'

Stirling retreated, beaten by her unexpected calm aggression.

'It's errr … it's the sort of bloody cornet kids are give when they start.'

'Right, Stir. Think hard. What other explanation have you got for a beginner's cornet being in the house, other than me taking on a beginner fancy man?'

'Errr.'

'You can do better than that. How many people live here?'

'Errr.'

'Let me help you, Stir. Two. And how many people can play a trumpet?'

'Errr. One. Errr. Me.'

'And now we're going to have two playing. Or one playing and one learning. Right?'

Dolores turned back to her onions and chopped viciously.

'Errr … Can I ask summat?'

There was a long silence. Gradually the silence softened and Dolores' back began to take on a mollified look. Time and weary custom were the active mollifiers, Dolores having lived with Stirling for almost thirty years.

'So I can ask?'

The silence now seemed familiar, not unusually cross.

'Am I daft, or do you mean you're learning t'bloody cornet?'

Dolores swung round. Stirling was relieved to see that a very small smile was beginning to bend her straight mouth. She said nothing, just looked at him, nodded and turned back to her onions.

'Errr ... Why?' he was bold enough to ask.

'Because I fancy it. A damn sight better than I fancy another fella, anyway. So I'm taking lessons.'

'Errr?'

'From Bernard, since you ask. He's a good teacher. You always said he were rubbish.'

'Yes, but I didn't mean it. It's like saying t'beer glass isn't filled right to t'line. Just summat to say.' There was a long pause. Dolores swept the chopped onions into a pan. 'Are you 'oping to join t'band?' There was controlled horror in Stirling's voice.

'Bernard says I should be ready to join in a month.' Dolores let the words fall softly, like oil on the flame of Stirling's anxious mind. 'You need another back row cornet, you were saying.'

'Bloody 'ell.' Stirling could bear no more.

He turned and went weakly out of the kitchen which smelt deliciously of frying onions. He had to support himself against the door jamb as he went. Slowly.

'He was really flummoxed. It were lovely,' Dolores said later that evening to Annie. 'He believed me about the month.'

'Why are you learning? I'd have thought that if you'd been keen you'd have learnt years ago. And why didn't you tell him you were going to learn?'

'It's not so bad for you. You're more important to Horny than the band but the band comes first with Stirling. It's, well, it's a sort of a family, really, and I felt this year that I wouldn't mind belonging.'

She looked at Annie, knowing that she was much too honest to argue. It was true. Both knew it.

Later, when Annie had gone, Dolores stood with her hands in warm, bubbly water meaninglessly washing over and over again the cups and plates she and Annie had used. Why was she learning the cornet, she wondered. What she'd said to Annie had been true but there were deeper reasons if she dug for them.

Since Maggie had married and gone Dolores had envied Stirling. He mattered to twenty five other people, and he mattered three times a week. Sometimes more. There was a better reason for him to get up on those days than earning money. Those men in the band all worked together and suffered together, as well as having a good time in the pub. That part of it, the jokes and the pints, was nothing in comparison with making music, she was sure.

She sat down, wet hands still foamy and thought a little sadly. She knew there was no realistic possibility of her getting to a stage where she could play with Harden Moss Band, but she supposed she might just make it to the junior band. Would she have the courage to try? There'd be twenty odd kids laughing at her when she went for an audition. It would take guts, she thought, and laughed at herself. Really, she might as well give the cornet back to Bernard.

Then she thought again. She was giving herself a chance to belong to a group of equals, struggling to do something well, together. Something difficult, unselfish, respectful of the other players. She could recognise this from knowing Stirling. And she'd always liked the music the band made. Every Saturday night the concert was colourful and people were happy to listen, and the men who were creating the music were even happier.

Goodness, she well knew there could be magic made. After all, she'd fallen for Stirling because of the solo he played, all those years ago.

She sat so long that her soapy hands dried and she didn't notice until the front door banged and Stirling came in, a cold freshness entering with him.

'You're early. Nothing wrong, is there?'

'No. No, nowt. I was just sitting there in the rehearsal tonight, thinking. I reckon it's a bloody good idea that you learn t'cornet. Tha can't be much worse than half back row, given that thi teeth are all thi own. That's not true of half back row. I'll support thi all the way. I'll even give thi lessons.'

He paused significantly.

'If tha'll mek meat and tatie pie twice a week instead of just once. Is it a deal?'

Sponsors

It was early March, nearly time for the band's annual general meeting and the committee was worried.

'But 'ow can us manage? All right, the Christmas collection bought us them timps but we need a new bass trombone at t'very least,' said Tommy.

'And t' baritone sitting next to me sounds a bit bloody rough,' added Stirling. 'Mind you, that's just Jaspar.'

'We all know that our own instruments need money throwing at 'em,' said Reg who was chairing the meeting, 'but t'band just 'asn't got it. We've to buy the parts for next year's area piece, there's us entry fees, subsidy for t'coach, tarting up t'uniforms ...'

'Aye, Reg. We've all been in the band long enough to be able to add up,' said Horny. 'Err ... has anyone thought we might get sponsorship?'

'Bloody 'ell. 'Oo'd want to sponsor us?' Stirling voiced the opinion of them all. Not one of the bandsmen there could imagine a firm paying towards a band which he was good enough to play in.

'Nay, don't be such a lot of nellies,' said Horny. 'We represent the village, don't we? We turn out at Christmas. Midnight in the square then Christmas morning round the streets. People say it makes Christmas.'

'Aye, and we aim to get ourselves legless by Christmas dinner-time, goin' collectin' in't pubs,' added Tommy.

'And play for t'chapel, Whit Friday.'

'And on Remembrance Day.'

'And for weddings, unless we're asked not to.'

'And every bloody Saturday for t'concert in t'bandroom.'

'So if we think sponsorship's a good idea, who do we finger?' asked Widget.

'There's t'Garden Centre.'

'Aye, they've been rakin' it in,' said Widget to harmonised groans.

'Bloody good idea. We could tell 'em we'll play in their caff ... if they don't give us money,' said Stirling.

'Well, we can always start with them, an' go on to t'mill, then finish off at t'undertakers,' suggested Reg. ' 'Oo do we send?'

Bernard as a schoolteacher felt that he had a duty to introduce some dignity into the quest for money, and the committee decided that Horny should bring to the task his years of experience in as many different jobs as the valley could offer. Since nobody else was willing to go.

'So go on, then, what 'appened?' asked Stirling as he and Horny walked down towards the pub.

'I'm thirsty. Wait until I've got a pint,' said Horny.

'You know 'ow to drag out t'bloody agony,' complained Stirling.

'Well, strictly speaking I ought to wait till next committee meeting.'

'Bloody 'ell, Horny. What's all this playin' 'ard to get? You couldn't bear lasses 'oo did that, as I recall. You couldn't wait. Instant bloody gratification was what you craved.'

'I take my pleasures leisurely now, Stirling. Make 'em last. It's called maturity.'

'Hey up, we're 'ere. D'you want to wait for your bloody pint, to mek it taste better? Just watch me drink for t'fust round. It's called maturity.'

Urgent thirst quenched, Horny put down his glass, sighed, wiped his lips with the back of his hand and said 'That's better.'

'Are we rich, then? 'Ow much?'

'Well. We decided, Bernard and me, that we'd practise on the mill. Not a lot of hope there, we thought, because it's all split up into bits and nobody's really what you might call coining it in. So we made an appointment to see the chairwoman of the co-operative that runs it. Nice lady she turned out to be.'

Horny took a long absent-minded drink, his eyes slipping into reminiscent mode.

'So? What did this nice chairlady say?'

'Nowt. No dosh. But ... err ... she's coming to hear the band next Saturday.'

'Honestly, Horny, you're not fit to be out on your bloody own. Hang on, you weren't on your own. What was yon schoolteacher doin' while you were workin' on chattin' 'er up?'

'Bernard's stomach had gone into freefall. Think it were nerves, myself. Spent most of his time in the loo.'

'So you got nowt out of t'mill. No, you've likely got summat if Annie doesn't hear about it; t'band's got nowt out of t'mill. Where next?'

'Bernard decided to try the undertakers. We've had such a clean, dry spell of weather that we reckoned their business hasn't been booming, so Bernard thought that they might look at anything in the nature of a new sort of enterprise'

'What enterprise? 'E's not offering 'em t'bloody band, is 'e? 'E doesn't expect a take-over, surely. Just imagine us: Harden Moss Band - We'll Be Pleased to Play at Your Funeral. Cremations a Speciality. We'd 'ave to get a list of music for punters to choose from. *Hole in the Ground. Firebird* or *Ritual* bloody *Firedance* might be better.'

'Don't be daft, Stirling. Any road, Bernard talked to the manager this time and I just sat there.'

'You didn't fancy your chances wi' Eddie, then?'

Horny ignored this. 'Bernard started in with the history of the band. How it were formed eighty seven years ago or whatever it were, how we moved up into second section in 1932 and down again three years later. He's still a teacher after all and obsessed with facts. Eddie's eyes were glazing over after a quarter of an hour ...'

Stirling interrupted,' ... and don't we know those glazing sessions? Eddie were lucky. Only quarter of a bloody hour.'

'Be fair, Stirling. Bernard used to have to tie you and me down to make us stay still. And did we ever concentrate? What can you remember of what he used to try and teach us?'

'Err ... 'E taught us to hide our feelings, lie, cheat ... not a bad education, when you think about it.'

'So after half an hour Eddie woke himself up and said thank you but no thanks. So we had just time to get to Mossies Garden Centre. I like that place. Smells good.'

'Any nice ladies there? Or did you try to talk about bloody sponsorship?'

'We'd rung up and arranged a meeting with the manager. Ten minutes, he said he could allow us. We went in and Bernard started his spiel about the story of the band - he'd obviously written it all out and learnt it. Luckily his stomach decided to help us. Soon as he'd excused himself I jumped in.

' "Have you been to one of our race nights?" I asked him. I told him about champagne for the owners, and how we name the horses. "I can just see Mossie running", I said, "and everybody cheering.

' "We get a right good turn out," I told him. "And we have a concert every Saturday. Can't you imagine a banner up above stage, with all the audience wondering how to spend their next weekend and reading 'Mossies Garden Centre' all night." I went on. You'd have been proud of me, Stir. Lucky we have green jackets. "Marching through streets, with Garden Centre on us banner in us garden green uniforms," I told him. Clinched it. Bernard came back just as he were saying he'd have to get approval from his board, but we walked out of there feeling rich.'

' 'Ow rich?'

'We reckon he might give us five grand, if we do a couple of special promotional concerts for the Centre. And whatever happens they'll let us have some potted plants for the concerts, if Bernard makes sure to mention the name of the Garden Centre when he's going on at the end.'

'By bloody 'ell. Five bloody grand. Should we bugger off to Amsterdam again?'

The Bandroom

A bright, mild April had come to the valley, and late afternoon sun stretched the broad shadows of the two steady-walking men who slowed as they climbed a steep, narrow little road, moors looming ahead, houses on one side and a field falling away on the other. Even their steady talking slowed.

They climbed, slowing even more, until they reached a building which clashed with the harmony of the village of Harden Moss. It was jammed between two straightforward terraces of tallish grey stone houses. Its red brick was a sour note and jarred with the shrill blue of its tile roof. The walkers turned up a couple of concrete steps and pushed through a swing door. Brass sounds met them, deep-bellied discords backing triple-tongued runs up the soprano cornet's octaves which sounded like tearing deckchairs. Horny and Stirling pushed through the noise to their own seats in the very centre of the band, facing Bernard, the conductor.

'Have you called a committee meeting after t'rehearsal?' Horny shouted across to Tommy, solo trombone. 'Have you any news?'

Bernard called the rehearsal to order. 'I'm sure we're all anxious to hear, Horny, but I suggest we wait until after the rehearsal, which is late starting because of you and Stirling. 'No. No excuses. I stopped listening to your excuses when you were in my first juniors' class!'

The music rampaged and sang. They clattered along with the *Washington Greys*, oozed with sugary sweetness through the jazzy bars of *The Entertainer*, and tripped out on their first outing with *Tryptich*.

Bernard worked with his usual dedication for nearly two hours, cajoling the few softer spirits while asserting his conductor's authority over the rest. The players blew themselves gradually into a familiar thirst. Pints in hand from the bandroom's bar, they reassembled in their band positions for the meeting.

Widget as top man was the band secretary. He waved a piece of paper silently and waited for the last person to be shushed. It was

Tommy, not born until 1954, shouting 'Hey up, letter from 'Itler, 'ave we? Peace in our time, is it?'

Then Widget spoke. 'This is the letter from the council which you've all heard summat about. Marked urgent, see. Let me read it.

To the Secretary of Harden Moss Band Club.

Dear Sir,

We regret to inform you that a serious blockage has occurred in the sewage system which serves the community of Harden Moss. Calculations based on our sub-terranean auto-investigative facility ...'

'Camera on t'end of a bloody rope,' explained Stirling, the plumber.

'... indicate,' Widget continued, 'that the said blockage is immediately beneath your bandroom. Due to the public health implications for the community it is imperative that the situation be remedied with the utmost urgency. We therefore inform you that we shall require the premises to be vacated for a minimum of two days from 14th April. We apologise in advance for any inconvenience.

Yours faithfully,

T. Willing, Sanitary Inspector.'

'Bog standard letter, I suppose,' snorted Horny. At the word 'inconvenience' half the band, those whose cars were parked in the road outside and therefore lived away, exploded with laughter, while the others muttered in agreement with Stirling's, 'Inconvenience. We know's all about bloody inconvenience. I've had nowt but bellyaching from our Dolores for a bloody week.'

'Yes, Stirling, but what is the band going to do? Are we going to let them rip up our floor?'

'How the bloody 'ell else are they goin' to get at their sewers, Bernard? A bloody teacher should be able to understand.'

'Just dig, will they? Picks and shovels?'

'Oh,' said Horny. 'I see what you're getting at, Bernard. If they're going to do the job in two days, they'll have to have mechanical diggers and whatnot.'

'Aye, an' to get them into't' bandroom they'll 'ave to tek t'roof off! Day after tomorrer!' concluded Tommy with the band chorusing in horror as they realised the destruction to come.

Widget's attempt to delay the devastation was like a worm trying to hold back a stone crashing downhill. By eight in the morning of April 14th a mechanical digger was lumbering past Stirling's front window. He rang in sick. So did Horny, Tommy, Reg and Widget. They watched as the digger stopped and inspected the concrete steps up to the bandroom then turned away and lumbered back home. First round to them and not a shot fired.

Next day, when the same group saw a mobile crane blot out the daylight they tried to have another day off work.

'Same problem as yesterday, is it?' asked each boss. 'You get in here now to work or come and collect your cards.'

So the bandsmen's wives found themselves suddenly struck down with blinding headaches and severe diarrhoea. Horny and Stirling arrived at their homes that evening after work to find bright-eyed expectant women waiting for them, mouths in gear.

'Anything happened?' Horny asked Annie in number 20.

'Another bloody waste of a day, were it?' enquired Stirling of Dolores along the street in number 28.

Annie pushed Horny down on to an armchair and sat on his knee. 'Just wait till you hear,' she said.

Three houses away Dolores sat at one side of her kitchen table and pointed Stirling to the chair opposite.

'Well,' she started, 'that crane had real trouble gettin' round the corner into Bandhole Lane. It were far too wide. What happened in the end were that it sort of trod on the wall into Hinchliffe's field. Me and Annie and Widget's Josie were there watching. Old Hinchliffe came charging across the field and yelled at the driver that if one of his cows got hurt he'd sue council.'

'So what did bloody crane driver do?'

'Well, just at that moment a diddy little digger came round the corner. Pretty little thing it were, very clean and yellow.'

'Don't be so daft. 'Ow can you call a bloody digger pretty?'

'Well, sweet, then.'

Meanwhile Horny had learnt about the crane's arrival and Annie had almost reached the point when the real disaster began.

'He didn't seem bothered about the wall,' Annie said. 'I suppose a crane driver gets used to knocking things down, so he started lifting his crane arm and sort of scraping the hook on the end of it down the roof, until the slates began to slide. Then he and the digger driver climbed up and chucked the loose slates off ...'

'Aye. I reckon he'd be exposing the metal beams.'

'Yes, that's right, and then he used the hook to pull one beam away and make a hole big enough for the digger to drop through. There was a crowd of us by then, and Josie went to get a flask of tea. And a couple of beers for the crane driver and the digger man.'

'What? Widget's missus giving consolation to the enemy? Never!'

'Well, they seemed all right. They were just following orders, Horny.'

'That's what the nazis said. Anyway, you fraternised with the enemy and then what?'

Dolores continued telling her tale to Stirling. 'He picked up that little digger like a baby picks up a cuddly toy ...'

'You're too bloody sentimental, you,' grumbled Stirling.

'... and he tried to swing it over into the bandroom.'

'But when he had it dangling,' said Annie to Horny, 'the whole cab of the crane began to swing round. Downhill, with the digger dangling from the arm. I saw the man's face in the cab as it swung past me and he looked desperate. Then the tracks of the crane began to sort of shuffle down the lane with the digger swinging from side to side. We'd all climbed down into the field by now ...'

'Must have jumped 'is bloody dog clutches,' said Stirling to Dolores. 'An' the weight of the thing swinging must have pulled the bloody crane forward.'

'The first swing took the digger straight through the wall of the bandroom,' Annie said, 'and the whole front collapsed, in slow motion ...'

'That little yellow digger was still swinging from side to side, pulling the cab behind it, like a pullalong toy ...'

'There was a line of cars parked,' said Annie.

'And the digger sort of swung and bounced right along the line,' said Dolores. 'It was like a kid in a playground with a ball - bounce against the wall, bounce against the ground, bounce against a red Escort,'

'That'd be Wally's,' said Stirling, 'Cleaned it every Sunday. 'Is pride and joy. Been saving up for that for years.'

'Then it flattened an Astra ...'

'Aye, young Battye's. Just bloody M.O.T'd last week 'e was tellin' me.'

'Then there was this old black one. I couldn't tell what it was.'

'Never. It didn't bloody hit that black one. Poor sod's nobbut just finished restoring it. A classic bloody car. A bloody British institution, the Morris Minor. A flat minor it'll be now, I suppose.'

'And the noise,' continued Annie, 'was amazing. Really exciting. Pity the band can't make a noise like that. But that's not all.'

'You can't go out and look yet,' said Dolores to Stirling. 'You haven't heard the worst bit. What happened later. You didn't smell anything when you got off the bus, did you? Mind you, wind would've been blowing the other way. And we've all spent ages washing this afternoon. After.'

'After what?' Stirling asked.

'Whatever next?' asked Horny.

'Do you remember when we saw that fountain in Lake Geneva?' Annie said. 'A great tall plume of water all glistening and beautiful in the sun? Well, this wasn't water, but it was as tall, or it looked it when you were standing right underneath it.'

'It was like a pretty multi-coloured peacock's tail,' explained Dolores, 'opening out suddenly from inside the walls of the bandroom. The sun was shining on it and it was really lovely - until you smelled it and realised what had happened.'

'Then the plume started spreading and falling. The stink! I can't tell you.'

It was a cheerful night in the pub. Ted Hinchliffe, the farmer, was celebrating his good fortune.

'That little squirt, Willing, lived up to 'is name. No haggling over cost of a new wall. And it's been fallin' down for years.'

The digger driver and the crane driver were enjoying free pints from the band.

'Pity you 'ad to knock the whole building down,' said Widget, 'but there was obviously no other way to get down and sort out that sewer.'

It took the council only eight and a half weeks to erect a glorious new stone-clad acoustically-designed bandroom having hired the plans used by Brighouse and Rastrick. The stated intentions of the population of Harden Moss, to sue for compensation and damage to health, unless the bandroom was replaced, proved to be a wonderful incentive.

Memories

Horny and Stirling had the new bandroom to themselves. They spoke in low, reverent tones.

'Bit bloody good this, eh, Horny?'

'Beautiful. Fancy us, little Harden Moss Band, having a new, clean place, near as fine as Briggus's.'

'Aye, and they had to have a bloody hit on pop charts to pay for theirs. Let's just hope the acoustics aren't too perfect.'

'Why?'

'Well, you daft bugger. If t'audience can't hear too well, they won't know when we're blowing bum notes. And a bit of sound bouncing round t'walls can help.'

'Anyroad, we won't know till we blow in it, will we? I don't remember when I looked forward to a rehearsal as much.'

'What's your favourite memory of t'old place?' Stirling asked as they started walking with hushed steps across the floor to the stage where the chairs stood ready for them.

'Hard to say. Memories jumble up from when we first started as lads, with Bernard. Harden Moss Junior Band. Really, I suppose, he was just giving us summat to do to keep us from thinking up more evil tricks to play on him when he was teaching us in school.'

'An' we enjoyed ourselves so well in t'band that we wouldn't bloody risk bein' chucked out.'

They sat, gently, in their own chairs, facing across the conductor's stand towards the invisible audience. The silence gathered and hung like a first note waiting to be played as they thought.

Horny looked at Stirling, trying to see in him the boy of forty years or so earlier. Funny to think of the skinny kid in short trousers and a fair-isle pullover packed away inside the broad shape of Stirling. Comfortable, that was how Stirling always looked to Horny.

'Could be just that he's been part of my life for so long,' he thought. 'In some ways he hasn't changed. Same light eyes. Same ordinary colour hair, a bit grey now as well, though, what's left of it. It was always very short when he was a kid. It would be that mother of his kept it so short. She used to hate him knocking around with me. Told my mam I was a bad influence on her boy ...'

Stirling interrupted his thoughts. 'My fust memory's definitely when we won t'bloody pools,' he said. 'Brilliant, that were. So exciting. A lot of money for lads like us an 'Tommy. And it were your idea, Horny, to go on tour, using some of our win to pay for the coach and beer.'

'Mainly beer, as I remember. That takes us back some years, Stir. We had a committee meeting to discuss it, didn't we?'

'And everybody was mad keen to go, so long as we could go wi'out female attendants, so to speak. And you said that you knew some bird in Amsterdam ...'

'Yes, I certainly remember that one. Lise ...'

'Trust you to recall t'lass. An' she got us cheap rooms.'

They both sank back again into comfortable silence as they remembered. Stirling smiled to himself. They'd asked Lil, the band's barmaid, to come. She'd deserved a treat. She'd looked after them all, some of them very well, he thought, glancing at Horny who was smiling too. 'She knew us bloody better than our own mothers in them days,' thought Stirling. 'And wasn't she gorgeous? The perfect barmaid. Big, blonde and busty, quick with the talk and quick with the beer.'

'Remember that we took poor old Bernard, though 'e 'adn't put owt into t'pools?' he said aloud. 'Against 'is principles, happen.'

Horny's thoughts were running along the same lines. 'Or his mother's. She's always been a mean old misery of a woman. When he were living with her Bernard never drank, never stopped out late, never spoke to women'.

'And every man in t'band knew 'ow 'e felt about Lil. Poor bloody sod. Used to make moon eyes at 'er while 'e was tucking 'is scarf neatly across 'is chest under 'is overcoat, just like 'is mother taught 'im. An' e' always 'ad to go straight 'ome after rehearsals to make 'is mother's bloody cocoa!'

'He was getting on then. Must've been well into his thirties. I'd been having a bit of a cuddle with Lil the night before we went, and she told me that she thought she might make a play for him on the trip.'

'Tough proposition, that. A bit like playin' a sardine that someone's tekken out of its tin and 'ooked on your bloody line.'

They laughed in a kindly way.

'D'you remember the raffle on the coach?' Stirling said. 'I'd nearly forgotten that. And we rigged it so that the second baritone, that young lad, eighteen and looked bloody twelve, what were his name? Anyroad, so e'd win. Mind you, until we saw 'ow things were goin' wi' Bernard and Lil, Bernard 'isself were a serious candidate'

Their memories dwelt on the tour round the red light district, the band shopping for the most beautiful girl. 'She were gorgeous,' thought Stirling. 'I can still picture 'er. Wonder if anything in the lad's life since 'as lived up to that.'

Horny was laughing. 'And the rest of us were well tanked up and we split into teams and started racing, leapfrogging the bollards over the little bridges ...'

'Aye, wi' crowds of Dutchmen cheerin' us on by t'end, and then Reg got stuck, and it took three of us to pull 'im off. He were older than us in them days. We've bloody caught up wi' 'im.'

'He weren't just the same for the rest of the trip. Poor Reg.'

'Poor Reg nothing. 'Is team of basses bought a terrace of 'ouses wi' their cash, and they're still fleecing poor bloody students. Like young Tim the timps.'

'So everybody got summat good out of the win. Trombones got enough to drink themselves daft for the rest of their days, young what's his name got a beautiful memory, Reg and the basses got an income, and Bernard got Lil. And a family to follow. What about you, Stir? What would you say you got out of the money?'

Stirling never hurried the thinking process. He tilted his chair back, looked up at the acoustically designed ceiling and pondered. Finally he lowered his chair to the floor.

'It were me fust time abroad, and to go wi' mates, and have fun, that were brilliant. T'money were great because it let me do that.'

He thought some more.

'But when we got 'ome our Dolores saw me as a rich man and that were the end of bloody freedom. Which I suppose made that trip even more special. You?'

The rest of the band were starting to arrive with shouts of astonishment on seeing Stirling and Horny, famous for being late, already in their places.

Stirling looked at Horny sitting there on his right, still with some of the good looks which had made his life as a legendary letcher so easy when he was young and which had helped to make his nickname inevitable, still the friend who had always led their joint enterprises.

'Go on,' said Stirling. 'Tell us. What did the money mean for you?'

'I've been trying to think, and I don't know,' said Horny. 'I bought this instrument. I took out a few girls. I bought a nice car to take them out in. What a waste. All that dosh and it made no real difference to my life.'

Bernard walked in, looking around him, his face shining with the same brightness of anticipation that Stirling and Horny had seen on every other face. Most of the band were in their places, rustling with excitement, instruments cradled, mouthpieces warming within lips. Stirling, who had been remembering the younger Bernard, so easily wooed and won by Lil, saw the neat white hair and the tired lines on the face which Bernard raised to the band almost with shock. But the voice was the same.

'Gentlemen,' he began with familiar, formal pomposity 'This very pleasant room will not of itself improve our playing, and we have a lot to do in order to be ready for our first concert of the new era.

'As a band with high aspirations to elevate ourselves from the third into the second section, we must get to work. I have heard it said that in order to do well a band must look good or sound good. Our splendid new bandroom helps with the first. Let us now endeavour for the second. We will begin, appropriately, with the familiar arrangement of part of Dvorak's *Symphony from the New World* with which we opened the village hall ...' and as he raised his baton he looked round his semi-circle of expectant men much as he had looked round at the boys in his first junior band so long ago.

That night, after the first rehearsal in the new era, as Bernard had called it, Stirling lay awake. He was thinking with a kind of regret of those glorious days of freedom in Amsterdam, when the whole world had been his for the grasping. It had been fun, as he'd said to Horny. He turned his head and looked at the solid shape of Dolores sleeping beside him. He'd been so flattered when she'd made it clear to everybody that she'd chosen him. Dull old Stirling. Plumber's apprentice. It had really started after one of their concerts when he had played a solo. What had he played? Yes, of course, *The Ash Grove*. She had been sitting with some of the other lasses from the mill and they'd got noisier and fuller of laughter as the evening wore on. Every young lad in the band was noticing them and pretending to pick out the one he'd make a pass at later. He remembered that he'd had his eye on a tall slim girl with a floating mass of dark hair. The opposite of Dolores, really.

When they'd finished the last piece and the band walked through the audience back to the little room where they left their instruments and uniforms, this small oblong lass sitting at the same table as his dark girl had caught hold of his sleeve. Stirling smiled as he looked up at the invisible ceiling. She'd said something nice about his playing and asked if he wanted a drink. Well, he was never one to turn down a drink, even then, and it would have seemed rude if he hadn't spent the rest of the evening with her and then walked her home. She felt compact and full of electricity when he put his arms round her for a goodnight kiss. And she was the one who asked if they were going to see each other again. What could he say? as he told Horny. It all seemed to happen naturally after that. She made it easy for him to accept what she suggested. Was he just simple? he wondered. He hadn't intended to wed her but it seemed she'd made the decision. Horny had worried and talked to him. It's for the whole of the rest of your life, he'd told him. If you feel strongly enough about her then it'll work out. If you don't then don't let it just happen. And he had let it happen.

He listened to her breathing. He wondered how important she was to him in comparison with the band and he knew with complete certainty that the band was in the foreground of his life and Dolores stood square and solid in the background. Should it be like this? he thought briefly then dismissed the notion. 'Thinking's Horny's trick. I'm getting too much like him.'

Still, she had been a good enough wife to him. After the tricky first year, when she had seemed to expect him to give up his playing and stay at home with her every night, life had pegged on peaceably enough. Maggie had appeared, their only child, as square and determined from birth as it seemed were all the women in Dolores' family. Dolores' own mother had married a man with a sense of humour and a will as strong as her own. He'd insisted on the name Dolores, so out of place for a girl likely to be a mill-worker in a small Pennine village. Her brothers and sister were called decent, squareish names. Maybe being named Dolores had made her a bit of an odd one out, it suddenly occurred to Stirling.

She hadn't become one of the band's enthusiastic supporters, following them to jobs and contests, but he supposed she enjoyed the Saturday concerts. She was nearly always there, sitting in her usual place. Could have been worse, he thought, hunching the duvet round his ears as he rolled on to his side.

Horny had got out of bed and was sitting in a chair by the bedroom window, looking at the June night. It was almost as bright as day, as so often in the midsummer north, and the moon was high. He looked at the one o'clock street, silent, with only a solitary cat going gracefully about its life. Annie was sleeping as she always did, as she always did everything, with absolute conviction. He knew without looking that she would be lying on her back, her head turned a little to one side, hair flung energetically across the pillow and her arms curved up and round her head, fingers clasped. He smiled at the night outside then pulled the curtain across the window and slid silently into bed.

She half woke and turned her head towards him, and she too smiled, in her sleep.

Charisma

'Wonder why Bernard's excited?' murmured Horny to Stirling.

' 'Ow d'you know 'e's ...' Stirling started to say then he looked at Bernard. 'Oh aye,' he continued. 'If I hadn't known Bernard since I were five I'd say 'e'd been on the cordial. 'Is white 'air sets t'colour off nicely. I'm not saying I've never seen a face as red, but I 'aven't since our Maggie went to a fancy dress party as a tomato.'

'Did she win a prize?' asked Horny.

'No. A bloody leek won. And t'bloody leek were Reg's daughter. She were allus long and skinny were Reg's lass. And people said the green 'air suited 'er. It 'ad to, any road. She couldn't wash it out.'

'Hey up, we're about to be told,' said Horny.

'Gentlemen,' Bernard began in a voice which vibrated like an old-fashioned cornet soloist. 'I am delighted to tell you that an old friend of mine ᵒ'

' 'E's gettin' bloody redder,' said Stirling. 'Beats Maggie the tomato now.'

'... in fact, a lady I was at college with ...'

'Watch out. Get ready to duck,' said Horny. 'He's going to explode!'

'has agreed to come as semi-professional conductress to take us to the Holmfirth contest.' Bernard took a deep breath and relaxed a little. The fascinated band watched his skin tone reduce in intensity from puce to crimson and back to scarlet. 'She has won many prizes for the orchestra and the school bands she directs in Surrey and has agreed to give us the benefit of her wisdom - free- for old comradeship.'

As he said the last words the men nearest Bernard moved back a little as if from a roaring bonfire.

The post-rehearsal talk focussed largely on Bernard and the woman.

'It'll be entertaining to watch Lil and this lass wi' Bernard,' said Reg.

'Now I look at Reg, I can see his resemblance to a leek. Must run in the family,' muttered Horny to Stirling.

'I'm reet lookin' forward to us next rehearsal,' said Tommy.

Two days later they were all early, sitting blowing tricky bits as they waited for Bernard and his companion.

'She's 'ere!' said the sop player, his voice rising and cracking under the stress of the moment exactly like his notes. Instruments were held absently to lips as Bernard opened the door of the bandroom to usher in a woman. She was nearly as tall as Bernard and looked young.

'Can't credit that they were at school together,' said Reg as Bernard and his guest crossed towards the stage ...

'Nay, be fair,' said Horny. 'It were music teachers' training college. Our Bernard went when he'd been teaching for - ooh - near twenty year, I reckon. Being refreshed, they said.'

Bernard hummed and erred his way through an embarrassing introduction. Stirling watched the woman's face as he was speaking. She smiled, seeming to accept Bernard's awkwardness as an endearing part of his personality.

'Can't imagine this 'un bein' a teacher. Far too nice,' Stirling thought.

Then she spoke. 'I'm Meg,' she said.

Stirling stopped listening to her words and just heard the music of her voice. He came round as she was saying, ' - though bands in the south truly are not nearly as good as up north,' flashing a smile round them all. Stirling found himself grinning back. He retained an impression of dark eyes looking intently into his own, only for a tiny fraction of a second, but they seemed to burn into his head - or was it his heart? He couldn't be sure.

'Just to help me to find my bearings, I'd like us to play a hymn tune, and since I need all the help I can get,' again the gleaming smile, 'we'll have the *Old Hundredth*.'

The rehearsal progressed. The band had done several hours' worth of preparatory work renewing acquaintance with a former test piece, the *Alton Towers Suite*, so every man was reasonably confident about his notes and dynamics. After almost two hours, during which time they had worked without a break, and everyone with the exception of Stirling had forgotten that she was a woman and concentrated fiercely on his part, she put her baton down gently on her music stand and said,

'Thank you very much. That was most exciting. If this is third section banding, then I'm amazed at the difference between north and south. You obviously know your parts well. What I should like to do now is arrange for us, just us, just the band, to go together to Alton Towers. I'm ashamed to say I've never been, and it should help our interpretation. What do you say?'

The trip was arranged, most of the band taking a day's holiday.

The May day was pleasant but chilly and they had the place almost to themselves. They swirled on roundabouts and plunged down black holes, dizzied themselves on walls of death and yelled all along the corkscrew big dippers.

Meg, radiant and breathless, gathered them round her as they stood eating burgers. 'So we've shared the funfair bit,' she said. 'Now we'll wander around the gardens, before it gets chilly, and we'll finish off in the mansion.'

Stirling found himself, as if by chance, walking beside her along the garden paths. They looked silently at the beds of flowers.

'Err ...' began Stirling. 'Err.

Meg looked at him and smiled that amazing smile which spun candy floss strands around Stirling's heart.

'I thought you might like to hear summat about t'band. Y'know, about us who play in it, and some of t'things we've done. Or 'as Bernard told you it all?' he added hastily and dismissively.

'Bernie's given me some of the history of the band, of course, but nothing about you all. I'd love to hear,' said Meg.

Stirling felt that he was made of candy floss himself. With a huge effort he stopped himself from melting, and not looking at his companion he began.

'I reckon I'd best go back to t'start. Bernard set up a youth band wi' a few of us lads from school. We were right baduns for 'im, and I reckon 'e thought 'e might keep us under control if we 'ad summat we really wanted to do, like, an' 'e could say 'No band unless you do your work,' sort of thing.'

Meg was laughing already. Stirling's heart swelled.

'It were a long number of years ago when we won Littlewoods - pools, I mean. It really were a lot of money, an' we went on this amazing band tour. To Amsterdam. It were me fust trip abroad. We 'ad fun like I couldn't 'ave believed. Err ... Bernard and Lil got together on that trip.' He looked sideways at Meg's face. She was looking at him.

He felt his face flush and went on talking quickly. 'We've did some daft things, as a band, but they've been great things, too, somehow. 'Ave you ever 'eard of Peaseholme Park? It's a park in Scarborough where bands play on a sort of a little island, Sundays. It's a floating platform really, but there is an island, and … This, what I'm going to tell you, 'appened to us much later than Amsterdam, when we should 'ave known better. I was wed to Dolores and Bernard and Lil 'ad been married for a long time.

'Well, any road, we played on the platform and felt right proud, since the important bands used to play there. Lil were wi' us, and she 'ad on this bl ... this great big 'at. It somehow 'appened that we left 'er behind on t'island, and she sort of 'itched a lift in a canoe wi' this little lad. She were always a big woman and she wore this shiny gold thing which made 'er look bigger. I were really sorry for that little lad. Her 'at came off and fell into t'lake. Lil tried to reach it and when she leaned over ...'

Just at this moment Bernard came up to them. 'Now then, Meg,' he said, 'I think we should start making our way ...'

'Bernie, dear,' said Meg, laying a gentle hand on his arm. Stirling watched in fascination as Bernard's forehead swelled and darkened, and lumps that Stirling had never before noticed appeared on it like ripe Victoria plums. 'I just want to hear the end of this fascinating story. I'll join you shortly.' She turned away from Bernard and looked at Stirling with complete attention.

'Err ... ' said Stirling, his insides looping around on a roller-coaster which made it hard for him to think or speak. 'Me and Horny 'ad just got out of our boat on to t'bank when there was an almighty splash and the canoe was upside down, Lil 'ad disappeared an' all we could see were a little old dog paddling towards the 'at, and a commotion underwater like Nessie. Since me and Horny were nearest we dived in and swam over and tried to haul 'er out. Then all t'rest of t'band jumped in.' Seeing her smile and the beginnings of the words of retreat on her lips he went on hurriedly, 'and then there were the time we won through to t'National Finals. Aye. We played in t'Royal Albert 'All.'

'I didn't know that. How wonderful. You didn't win, of course, or I'm sure I'd have heard about it from Bernie.'

'No. It were sad, when I think about it. It was so important for us, and I lost it for t'band. They've never blamed me for it.' Horny was hovering, watching his friend with concern. 'Even 'im,' said Stirling. 'It were really me bottle.'

Now Bernard was coming again to drag Stirling's listener away.

'And when we 'ad the fight and won the pickled onion trophy bowl. And when Horny broke 'is ...' It was no use. She was gone, with a 'Thank-you for that,' and the sweetest of backward glances, so sweet that Stirling would unwrap the memory of it for the rest of his life to comfort sad moments or celebrate joyous ones.

Stirling never told Horny about the time he fell in love.

Modern Music

'Another?' asked Horny.

' 'Ow long 'ave we known each other?' answered Stirling.

'All right. Just being polite,' said Horny.

'Bloody 'ell. 'Ow long 'ave we known each other,' Stirling said again.

Horny came back to the table with two more pints, light froth just beginning to edge over the top of each glass and slide down the side.

'I'm wondering about this next concert programme,' he said as he sat down.

'Your trouble is you think too much,' said Stirling after taking his first long drink from the new glass.

'Yes, but Stirling, even you must have thought a bit about all this modern stuff Bernard's making us play. Not a tune in the whole lot. Who's going to stop in the bandroom on a Saturday night and listen to a bag full of spanners rattling around? And if we don't have an audience we don't have bar sales and if we don't ...'

'All right. Matter of fact, I like it. I surprise meself sometimes. It's bloody exciting.'

'It might be better for you. Flugel gets all the pretty bits. By the way, has it ever worried you?'

'What?'

'Spending the best part of your life with the pretty bits? Has it affected you?'

'It'll affect your teeth if you carry on casting nasturtiums like that. Any bloody road, we were talking about this modern music. And I like it. And the audience can't tell if your tuning's out, or you've clipped a note, so it's relaxing. Better than S.O.S. anyday.'

'Oh aye, same old shit.' Horny laughed. 'But how can you call it relaxing, when it's trying to make you think of *Intergalactic Battleships* or summat? If it's relaxing then composer's failed, hasn't he?'

'I tell you, you think too much. Tek life simply's my motto. A bloody good blow with me mates, enough noise to shake our lovely new bandroom's foundations, and an audience to give us a bit of appreciation at the end, that'll do me. So in't it enough for you? Go on, then, you daft bugger, what do you want from music?'

Horny drank slowly and put down his glass slowly. He leaned back in his chair. Stirling had forgotten his question when Horny finally spoke.

'I suppose I agree with what you said - mates, a good blow, making enough noise together to wake all those old bandsmen up on the hill there, and ... there's summat else. Don't you sometimes find you've got beyond being Stirling? You've forgotten who you are, just for a few moments. You're up there somewhere in glorious chords. It doesn't often happen, but when it does it's grand. Just now and then, when I'm managing to saw through *Poet Unpleasant* and I'm listening to me own music, then, maybe.'

'That'll be the day. They used to call t'piece *'Poet and Peasant'* until you started playin' it, you know.'

Stirling got up. 'My round,' he said.

The Triumphal March

Holmfirth contest was ending as magnificently as it always did, with a table, properly dressed in a cloth, carried on to the stage to be over-laden with silverware - cups and shields and trophies.

Stirling and Horny were leaning against the doors at the back of the hall, enjoying an unusual feeling of confidence. Their performance of The Alton Towers Suite had been cheered, of course, but then so was every band's performance. Supporters, and even ordinary members of the public who liked the warm company of friends and the music of local bands, honed and polished over weeks of extra rehearsals, brought their babies and flasks and packets of sandwiches and stayed in their seats all day. And applauded and cheered as part of the routine.

'Look there, Stir,' said Horny. 'Lil's gone and got changed for the awards. How about that!'

'By bloody 'ell, she's nearly hit t'right colour. Her tuning's a hair sharp, that's all.'

'We weren't today. That Meg did wonders for us.' Horny looked sideways at Stirling. 'Hey, we're starting. Raffle first.'

The master of ceremonies seemed to know everyone in the hall and the raffle continued interminably. Stirling and Horny drifted off into their own preoccupations, Horny admiring Lil's legs in their shiny green tights and Stirling looking at Meg where she stood beside Bernard.

' 'Aven't we got anyone with blue 475? No? Come on, everybody, look. Well then, mauve 139. Dear me. We sold the ticket. Somebody must 'ave it.'

Suddenly Bernard was asking, 'Is this mauve?' and setting off down the aisle, his white head was at the front of the hall, the master of ceremonies saying 'Are you coming to collect all the prizes, Bernard?' then he was beaming his way back carrying a large oblong tray, made festive by being wrapped in silver foil.

Lil held out her hands and the tray was plonked heavily on her lap. Heavily because it held several slices of gammon, a pound or so of sausages, half a dozen eggs, mushrooms, tomatoes and black pudding. A breakfast, donated to the raffle by H. Mitchell and Sons, Purveyors of Fine Meat.

The results were announced, kindly, as always.

'And third in section B, the band that played number 4, second in the section, band that played number one who will receive a cheque for fifty pounds, and the winners, who will receive the cup and the cheque for One Hundred Pounds, when Mr Whitehead 'as written it out. Up you come again, Bernard. Here we are. Harden Moss Silver Band.'

Stirling's eyes were on Meg's delighted face as he roared his exultation with the others.

Marks and awards continued to be handed out to untiring cheers and to bright-faced bandsmen and girls who leapt or stumbled up the steps to the stage to accept cheques and silverware with triumphant arms raised.

Suddenly it was all over and it was seven o'clock. Time for the march. Along the main road into the centre of Holmfirth, a sharp left at the traffic lights and down Victoria Street.

The band began to assemble in relaxed fashion outside the Civic Hall.

'Hey up, Horny. We're t'front band! Bloody 'ell. Winning band in us section, eh? What a responsibility.' Stirling nudged Horny. 'Pay attention to Bernard.'

'In fives, please, gentlemen. No, in fives. Fives, cornets. Tim, in the middle. You know what you do? You don't? Listen, then.'

Bernard's voice was rising.

'Bass drum, Tim, two beats to prepare us then two threes - bum, bum, bum - before we start playing.'

Horny nudged Stirling who was grinning behind his mouthpiece.

'We play the first eight bars before we move off on the left foot.' Loudly. 'Is -that - clear?'

Meg put a hand on Bernard's arm.

Lil was at the top of the Civic Hall steps and even from that distance she appeared to the band, watching in fascination from the road below, to swell. Her face darkened.

'What a way to finish a great day,' said Horny. 'A tussle for old Bernard by two powerful women. I'm on Lil's side. Anyone who can tackle a day like this and then march round the streets at her age wearing four inch bright green high heels and a matching mini-skirt has courage.'

Stirling said nothing. He couldn't. This would probably be the last time he'd ever see Meg.

'Look.'

Lil was making her cautious way down the steps, trying to look around the sides of the big silver tray she was carrying in both hands, in order to see where to put her feet. Her knees were pointing outwards and slightly bent. A small boy was climbing the steps against the flow. His face was a screen over which emotions chased each other like Tom and Jerry. Stirling and Horny saw his jaw drop, then he was frozen to the spot to be rapidly thawed as Lil reached him and snapped one easily lip-readable word. 'Move.'

Safely down to road level, Lil clipped her way rapidly to the front of the procession where Meg and Bernard were preparing to lead the march. Meg was carrying one enormous silver cup and a shield, Bernard held another taller slimmer cup and a second shield. Lil took up proprietary possession of Bernard's right side. She was carrying another silver item.

'What the bloody 'ell's that in 'er hands? Meg's got Best Band in Section, Best Conductor in t'Valley, Bernard's holding Best Bass Section and Best Holme Valley Band. So what's Lil ...?'

Delight overwhelmed Stirling.

'She's carrying t'breakfast. She mustn't have bloody noticed. Summat silver coloured and that's enough, feeling like she does.'

They were off.

Horny, his two horn henchmen and Stirling were in the second row of marchers, immediately behind the trombones. They could hear nothing but they saw Lil's mouth working in treble time as she marched in double time. Bernard's neck was very red. Stirling, heart aching, watched the back of Meg's shining hair.

Then the dog appeared. He was small, grizzled, wiry and very doggy. He lurked, at first, pretending to be with the crowd which lined the road as they marched and played. But he had an agenda of his own.

In a quiet moment Horny and Stirling could hear Lil's voice rising stridently. The applauders on the sides of the street stopped applauding to listen.

'How do you think I felt? Eh? Left behind! 'Ad you forgotten me?'

There was nothing plaintive in the last question. It was angry.

Then the real Tom and Jerry action started.

Lil was concentrating on what she was saying to Bernard and ignoring where she was walking so that one of her heels landed in a pothole. She rocked dangerously. As she tilted so did the silver tray and the covering silver foil allowed escape to the string of sausages which H. Mitchell, Purveyor of Fine Meat, had curled invitingly alongside the gammon. As Lil teetered on her stilts a tempting fat pink sausage dangled near the ground and the dog lunged.

His teeth met in the sausage and it was his. He pulled.

Lil was still off balance but like the dog she was a fighter. This trophy was hers. She had hold of one end of the string of sausages now, and she was baring her teeth at the dog.

The first lines of the band lost the beat and the step as Lil and the dog rocked and swayed in front of them and their part of the march tumbled into chaos.

The trombones in the first row began using their slides as weapons against the dog then solo trombone and bass trombone, working as a partnership, tried to chopstick him and toss him to the audience. But though he was old he was agile and cunning.

The small boy who had seen his first glimpse of adult heaven when he was climbing the Civic Hall steps had, like a squire of old, followed Lil and the marching band along the grey main street which was transfigured in his eyes, the walls blooming and the stones of the pavements blossoming. Now he saw his Lady of the Bright Green

Rose being attacked. It was his chance to prove his adoration and slay the dragon.

He rushed into the road and grabbed the old dog who was unprepared for assault from the rear. He whipped round and bit the dragon slayer.

Two things happened. The small boy grew up very suddenly and Lil fell backwards.

It was classic domino-tumbling. Lil fell against Bernard who was helpless, his hands full of the trophies of success. He fell against Meg. Stirling leapt to save her, crashing through the trombone players who had stopped dead in shock. Tim, hidden behind his drum and unable to see continued to bang the march beat, and the back row cornets found themselves trampling over their own front row and their conductor and his ladies then immediately they in turn were overwhelmed by the bass section. The triumphant winning bass section, blowing with eyes half closed in deep pride, so lost in their own sounds that they had failed to hear that the music in front of them had stopped.

The deportment adjudicator waited in his traditional spot in Victoria Street around the corner from the traffic lights. He had heard the first band approaching and his pencil was poised over his little yellow note pad when the sounds of *Punchinello* disintegrated into what sounded like war. He was a man accustomed to patience and order so he waited.

After what seemed like minutes, the march struck up again and the adjudicator re-poised his pencil.

Leading the march was a tall, curvy woman in bright green, holding hands with a small boy. Each carried a shield. Behind them the musical director and another woman marched in strict time, each carrying a trophy, and behind them came the green-uniformed band, all left feet in perfect unison.

At the very back a small, square, cross-looking woman was nursing a silver tray and kicking out at a small, wiry, cross-looking dog.

'Champion',' said the adjudicator to himself. 'It'll take a lot to beat that presentation,' and he wrote on his scrip, 'Harden Moss: Very well done. Thank you.'

Holmfirth Express: from our reporter:

'Harden Moss Triumph.

Harden Moss Silver Band led the march of the bands triumphantly around the streets of Holmfirth last Sunday, cheered by an excellent crowd enjoying the lovely weather. They were victors at Holmfirth Contest in the 'Own Choice' section, winning by a resounding three points with a sparkling performance of The Alton Towers Suite,'

Equality

Harden Moss Silver Band Club was its usual, noisy, cantankerous, blissful rehearsal self. Stirling sat on his chair, feet braced to support his spreading weight. He played a few warm-up notes, eyes on the door. Horny was late. The two of them usually walked up to the bandroom together but Stirling had been working away for a couple of days and had come straight from the job.

Their joint nephew struggled in with his E flat bass and squeezed into his place behind Stirling.

'Here, lad. Where's thi Uncle Horny? It's bloody late even for 'im.'

'Haven't you seen him, Uncle Stirling? Haven't you heard? He's chucked it.'

'What? He's done what? Chucked what? You don't mean 'e's chucked t'band? Niver. Bloody hell. Bloody hell. So what'll us do for solo bloody horn?'

Bernard the conductor looked slightly nervously round at his men.

'Err ... Good evening, gentlemen. Can we make a start? Now then, before we have a first go at our own-choice test piece, which, as you may know, the committee have decided should be *Year of the Dragon*, I have an announcement to make.'

He fiddled with the scores on the stand in front of him. His band looked expectant.

'Ermm ... You will no doubt have noticed that Cecil, our solo horn player, is not here.'

Bubbles of laughter escaped from all sides and murmurs of 'Never knew Horny had a real name,' and 'Bloody Cecil, eh. Haven't heard that since we were in juniors together. Wait till I see Horny.'

Bernard raised his mild teacher's voice. 'I very much regret that ... err ... when I informed Cecil of my decision to fill our empty first horn chair with ... err ... not to put too fine a point on it ... err ... with ... (in a rush) a girl in fact our daughter who will join us here very shortly, he handed in his verbal resignation. Quite forcibly.'

His last words were almost drowned in a rush of comments, chiefly 'Bloody hell' repeated regularly.

Bernard raised his less mild teacher's voice.

'Now then, gentlemen. We'll start with a hymn tune to get our instruments warmed up. Can you turn to *Deep Harmony.*'

A couple of hours later Stirling struggled through the crush around the bar to get back to his table.

'Well, Horny. 'Ere's your pint. Glad you came in to join us. Not a bad rehearsal. I tell thi what, yon lass can play a bit. She'd be a bloody good bumper-up for you. If you was to join us again, I mean.'

Their nephew, red-faced and bright-eyed, joined them. 'Hello, Uncle Horny - sorry, I suppose I should call you Uncle Cecil.'

'You do, lad, and you'll have blown your last note. With them teeth anyroad.'

'Isn't she gorgeous? That hair. All them fine plaits, like beautiful, wriggly golden snakes. It'll drive me crazy sitting just behind. I won't be able to concentrate on me pedal notes. I can't believe she's Bernard's daughter.'

'Aye, lad, but you never knew her mother as a young woman. Lil were sensational. I know she's a bit frightening now ...'

'Frightening? Horny, d'y'know what we're playing at contest? *Year of the bloody Dragon*! This is the year of the dragon and no mistake. You're not telling me that Bernard decided to put his daughter's pretty little bottom on a man's chair without being forced into it by his bloody fire-breathing man-eating wife.'

'Aye, but be fair, uncle. She is gorgeous, isn't she? Don't tell me you're too old to notice. And I know you did, Uncle Stirling. I've never seen t'flugel player have to bend down to pick up his mute so often. Or lean over and check dynamics on horn part. Six times I counted ...'

'That'll do. I was nervous; new player in the band. Go on, Horny. Say summat.'

'I reckon the band should call a committee meeting, next rehearsal.'

The committee members stayed comfortably in their seats after

Tuesday's rehearsal, grumbling mildly. 'Hey up, Horny. Now that tha's decided to re-join t'band 'ow about tellin' us why we're wastin' valuable drinkin' time.'

Horny spoke from his place in the centre of the semi-circle.

'Right, lads. Thanks for the chance to say me piece.'

He looked round at them all.

'D'you all realise how different things are going to be? You'll have noticed, no doubt, that we have an alien among us in t'band. A creature of a different species. The question is, do we accept this stranger in our midst, or do we give Bernard an ultimatum? Tell him that this is our band, we know who fits and who doesn't. We can all think of the disadvantages of having a female playing with us. Long bus rides to jobs, sharing dressing rooms, not being able to tell ... jokes ... you know. Yes, Stirling?'

'But think of the bloody advantages! Long bus rides to jobs. Sharing dressing rooms. And I reckon we should keep her on for the next contest, anyroad. I've been talking to your nephew. Ask 'im.'

'I'm sorry, Uncle Horny. I think we'll have to let them in sooner or later. And if that's the case this is the one who should come in sooner.'

'Nay, lad. Tha's only saying that because you fancy 'er. In't that right?'

'Well, I can't say I'd push her off if she sat on me knee, but that's not the main reason. You know the entertainment contest in three weeks is open adjudication.'

'So what, kid? So Walter will be sitting watching us mekin' fools of us-selves.'

'And you know where first horn sits?'

'Course I do. Alongside me. So?'

'Nay, uncle, think. She'll be facing the judge. I was at school with her. She used to drive the teachers crazy, wearing long black stockings just over the knee and short tight skirts. I've seen her sitting down. And their eyes when they tried not to look. Do you think Walter would pay any attention to our tuning with those long white thighs in his sights?'

There was a moment's silence then a general murmur of heart-felt agreement from the rest of the committee. Horny listened then sat thoughtfully.

'Who was that wench with snakes for hair, kid? You've been at school since me,' he asked.

'Medusa. Why, uncle?'

'She used to turn men to stone, didn't she?'

A second cornet spoke with suffering in his voice: 'Aye, and yon lass was starting to 'ave that effect on me!'

'Right.' Horny spoke decisively. ' If she can turn t'contest judge to stone so he doesn't notice Tommy's trombone solo in *Year of the Dragon*, then we'll give her free entry to join our club. Eh, lads? What do you say? Shall we give it a try? We've already got a dragon wi' our Lil interfering in the rightful decisions of the band. We might as well add another alien creature. I recommend to the committee that we be generous. Recognise that these are the early years of the twenty-first century. Let's be new men and move into the age of equality. And I'll buy you all a drink, just to christen our decision. All in favour?'

An hour later the committee strode with four pint firmness out into the Harden Moss night, all glorying in the astonishing goodness, generosity and justice of their hearts.

Images

Stirling put down one empty glass. 'By bloody 'ell, I needed that,' he said, picking up his second and supping a moderate inch. 'What d'ye reckon got into Bernard tonight? I think that were the most peculiar rehearsal I've ever been to.'

'He was talking funny,' agreed Horny, 'telling us to get ourselves into sort of feeling the music, not just playing. Let's ask the lad. Like as not he'll have an idea. He usually has.'

Their joint nephew was ready enough to join them.

'Well, Uncle Horny, Uncle Stirling. Did you find that rehearsal thirsty work? Me too. Want to find out what Bernard's daughter's been telling me? Pity me mouth's so dry, or I'd tell you.'

Stirling struggled up wordlessly and came back from the bar a minute or so later with a loaded tray. 'One for thee, Horny, one more for me and a half for the lad. Can't let him get into bad habits. Go on then, kid. Explain.'

'Well, apparently Bernard's had a school inspection, an Ofsted thingy, and the inspectors went on about how the best sort of learning and performance ties in wi' the imagination. So Bernard decided, his daughter said, that the band needed to let its imagination run wild a bit, and we might play better.'

'So all the bloody talk about the light of 'ope at t'beginning of *Morning* were to improve us fingering and dynamics, were it? Can you remember what he said, Horny?'

'He said he wanted us to see the sun rising like a young lass getting up out of bed, stretching her bare arms, shaking her tousled golden hair, he said, and ...'

'And I expected you to join in and add to the bloody description. You know all about young lasses getting out of bed, or into bed, anyway.'

'Used to, Stirling. And then he went on about how he wanted us to think of what hope meant for us. Did you do that?'

'Aye, I were still paying bloody attention then. It were early on and I can tell you my picture of hope were floating right clear in front of me eyes. It were a glass of bloody good ale, not too much head, just a bit of froth sliding down the side from the glass being so full. That were hope for me.'

'I didn't get the bit when he was talking about *Nimrod*. Did you follow lad? It went over my head, but since you've got nothing to do on the back row but blow a few oompahs, you can no doubt concentrate better than us workers.'

'Big part in *Nimrod* for basses, Uncle Horny. Listen, next time. He did go on a bit. Dark forests, and great creatures in the shadows, he said. And the hunter searching for a meaning to life.'

'Back to bloody ale again. I got into the taste of the beer for *Nimrod*. Made me play better - bloody faster, any road. The perfect beer, balanced between sweetness and bitterness. Cool, long and bloody marvellous. That reminds me, lad, isn't it thy turn to buy t'drinks?'

'But ...' Their nephew gave up the hopeless quest for fairness and carried the empty glasses back to the bar.

'It were love he were talking about for *Myfanwy*, weren't it?' asked Stirling. 'Just down your street, I thought to meself. But why the bloody 'ell was he going on about rhinoceroses?'

'What do you mean? He never mentioned them.'

'He bloody did. I'd sort of nodded off but I came to and he were talking about strange beasts with a single horn. I couldn't work out what bloody rhinoceroses had to do with love but I thought you'd be bound to know. Specialist, like.'

'You daft idiot. He were talking about the magical creature of dreams and stories - the unicorn! Glimpsed, and never caught, he said.'

'You seemed to manage to catch plenty. Hey up, here's our beer. About time too. Where've you bloody been? Ta, lad. We were just talking about love. 'Ave you an image for love, getting on so well as you are with Bernard's beautiful daughter?'

'Well, I did like Bernard's picture of a bird of many coloured plumage flying just out of reach of mortals.'

'And I expected Horny to choose the bloody phoenix, rising again and again and again. Come on, Horny, tell us. What's your image for love?'

Horny sat quietly for a little time.

'Well,' he said slowly, 'this is true. You know I've got a bush of some sort growing near my allotment shed, Stirling? Well, there's nearly always a robin sitting waiting for me on the end of a branch on that bush, and if I'm digging it comes and sits on the handle of me fork or somewhere near. I think of love as that little bird. Nice, pleasant song, company whenever I want it, there, but never a bother. I fair look forward to seeing that robin.'

Stirling pictured Annie, Horny's girl, and smiled. Just a perfect description of Annie. Lovely, he thought, which was the way he always thought of Annie.

'And it's got to be back to the ale for me,' he said aloud. 'Halfway down the perfect glass, happy, thirst-quenched, and knowing there's more to come. Last round's on me, lads.'

Bernard

Bernard was in his study, the desk in his daughter Dawn's old bedroom. He was writing his retirement speech.

'It has been my privilege to lead this school for almost forty years, leaving you all to your own devices (pause for laughter) only while I went for a refresher course some years ago. I have many fond memories of the old school, when the pupil register was three times what it is now and I was a lowly assistant teacher ...'

He put his pen down carefully parallel to the edge of his paper which was itself parallel to the edge of the desk and went downstairs. Lil was watching East Enders.

'Excuse me, my dear,' Bernard began, 'but may I interrupt your viewing for a few moments?'

Lil sighed and adjusted the volume control.

'Something has occurred to me and I wished to talk it over with you. Since I am retiring from school, the notion came to me that a simultaneous retirement from the band might be expected and I hoped for your advice. Do you think I should so do?'

'No, Bernard. Don't be daft,' said Lil and turned the volume up rather higher than it was before.

'Thank you, my dear,' said Bernard gratefully and loudly and went back to his desk and paper and pen.

But he did not at once start to write. He sat, looking out over the valley in which Harden Moss lay cupped and towards the hills beyond. His study window faced east, which was why he and Lil, in the morning flush of joy, had called their first child Dawn. Now, in July, the hills were still bright with sunlight.

Still such a hopeful picture, he thought and allowed his mind to drift over the times of hope which had lit up a life devoted to service. He supposed that forming the junior band had brought the first light to the dark days of his early teaching. The boys were wild and full of energy and his gentle formality had not held them in the restraint essential for him to teach.

Tommy and Horny and Stirling were the worst. How funny that I can no longer easily think of the last two by their given names, he thought, smiling. Cecil and Jack no longer fit them. Yes, the habit of forty-odd years is strong. Kind-hearted, comical children they used to be, but what a difference it made to me when they found a talent for brass playing.

Then of course Lil came into my life. My dearest wife. A glorious, golden-haired goddess when I first admired her from afar. Indeed I never allowed myself to consider the possibility that I could tell her of my love. His tired face relaxed into the memory of a smile. My dear mother knew nothing of how I thought of her. My lonely pillow was my only confidante. I remember one night well, as children so often recall the events just prior to a great event ...

The band had given one of its usual Saturday evening concerts, and had been even more ebullient and difficult to control than usual. It was almost with relief that he opened the door of the terrace house he shared with his mother and heard the inevitable greeting, 'Is that you, our Bernard?'

'Who else might it be, mother?' he muttered under his breath.

'Your cocoa's on the side of the stove; you might as well bring me a drink as well. You're late!'

'I hope you haven't been worried, mother. Some of the band wanted to buy me a drink after the concert.'

'A drink, did you say? It's not like you. I hope you weren't tempted to try alcohol.'

'No. I know it doesn't suit me. I just had two orange juices.'

'Eeh, our Bernard. That was a mistake. You'll be up and down all night. You're a martyr to your bladder.'

'I couldn't say no, could I? It would have been so rude.'

'Well, just see that you don't wake me, that's all. Staying out to this time. I call it selfish.'

'It's only a quarter to eleven,' Bernard said mildly.

Tommy, the band's bass trombone had always been a good-hearted lad, even though Bernard used to find it hard to stop him taking the littler ones' milk. And it was Tommy who had been first to insist that Bernard have a drink at his expense, even as he was struggling back to his table with a loaded tray - the first six pints for the trombone section, all three of them thirsty after an exuberant evening's work.

Bernard smiled at the memory. He picked up his pen, guilty at his self-indulgence in simply sitting and day-dreaming, then put it down again. The sunlight was beginning to leave the little town below him and the shades rising quietly up the valley sides held him entranced. He allowed himself to continue his reminiscing.

In his thoughts now he was again on the coach which the band had hired to take them to Amsterdam. By this time he had learnt of their pools win, and their delight in sharing it with himself - and Lil.

He shut his eyes and he could feel the prickly seat and smell the faintly fusty smell of the upholstery and the beer. He even remembered his thoughts. They had been concerned with his mother. He had replayed their last conversation which was itself a replay of many others.

'Eeh, our Bernard, I don't know how you can do this to your own mother. And me getting on as I am, too. You know full well that I'm sixty one next birthday.'

'Come on, mother. Mrs Battye is coming to stop with you.'

'Yes, and I know why. Nosy thing. She just wants to see how I keep my house. And what about you? How will you manage with nobody to give you freshly ironed underpants every morning? You know how easily you get a cold.'

'Now then, mother. You want me to enjoy myself, don't you?'

'Not if enjoying yourself means dirty things like stopping up late and drinking and ...'

'Excuse me. I hope you don't mind if I sit here.'

It was a soft, low voice which broke into Bernard's thoughts. Warm. Comforting. He'd imagined it speaking to him many times. He opened his eyes and looked up into Lil's smiling face bending over him.

'I've wanted to talk to you ever so often and I've never had a chance, being so busy behind the bar.'

Bernard felt a flush spreading from the freshly ironed parts of his body. What might life hold that could be better than this?

Bernard, older by thirty years now, white-haired, a tired old teacher, could still feel his old bones warmed by the thoughts of those few days in Amsterdam. He had proposed to Lil before they returned to the ferry. It was one of the ringing, trumpet-sounding occasions in his life when she said yes.

He heard his wife moving around in their kitchen. There were times still when he found it hard to believe that she would be there when he went downstairs and that she would share his bed. He sighed with the goodness of his fortune, saw that the sunlight was just leaving the tops of the hills and went to join Lil.

The following evening, in their little terrace house in the village in the valley, Dolores and Stirling had finished supper.

'Look, Dolores. There's a bloody great headline in't paper that says Retiring Local Teacher Heart of Village Band and it goes on about our Bernard! What d'ye think o'that?'

'Well, he's certainly done his best for you all, for how many years is it?'

' "Bernard Usher", it says, "talked to me in the deserted schoolroom of his little Harden Moss Junior and Infants School, which has an inscription over the door, Built In 1873." Oh, bloody 'ell. You read it out, will yer?' Stirling swished the Examiner across the table.

' "Bernard Usher talked to me in the deserted schoolroom ..." ' she read aloud ' " ... built in 1873. His teaching life has all been spent in Harden Moss and he well remembers joining the school when it served a flourishing community and he was the youngest of three permanent staff. He told me he was never ambitious, and he became head teacher of the school only when the intake of children had fallen so far that no new member of staff could be appointed after the retirement of the former head, Mr Brown, and Miss Norwood, who may both be recollected by some of our older readers. Those early days were happy days, he told me with a smile and the hint of a sigh. The youngsters used to bring their lunches to school, of course, and in the winter months there would be a line of pies and pasties balanced on the long black pipe that led from the old stove along the side of the room to warm it. In this way the children would have hot dinners, but of course hygiene regulations would not allow such a practice nowadays. He told me many fascinating stories of how teaching had changed, but I persuaded him - with very little difficulty, I may say - to tell me about the local band. Harden Moss Band." '

' 'Ere, hang on. I'd just gone to that school when Bernard came. Me and Horny give 'im some bloody bother, I can tell thi. Mr Brown the old head master was still there, an' he used to watch what was goin' on through the glass top of the door into Bernard's classroom. He'd look straight at Horny an' me, then he'd send for us. It were nearly allus me and Horny who got t'bloody stick so when that big grey head appeared our hands used to fair tingle.'

'Why? What did you do?' asked Dolores.

'Whatever we could. Just to mek life more interesting. We never could stand school. One of the best was when we drew lots and Horny won. He had to get up into under-drawing, crawl over joists in t'ceiling then stand as high up as he could and drop t'biggest, heaviest bloody book we could find just over Bernard's head. We thought it would be best if we did it when t'class was supposed to be quiet, so we waited till prayers. It were bloody appropriate that t'book were t'Bible, we thought after.'

'What did Bernard do?'

'Well, he were covered in plaster and dust. T'ceiling just about came down as well. Us kids were helpless wi' laughing. We all knew what Horny was goin' to do, so everybody was quiet when prayers started. Bernard must've thought he'd really got paradise on earth with all us mucky little buggers standing wi' our hands together like angels. And our eyes looking up towards heaven. Then a thunderbolt! Horny and me couldn't sit down comfortably for a week after. Not Bernard. Mr Brown. Carry on reading.'

' "Harden Moss Band … Bernard's eyes lit up with pleasure when he began to tell me about 'his' band. He had so many memories. The older members of Harden Moss Silver Band found it difficult to adjust to a young conductor at first, he said. He remembered occasions when some of the well-established players used to advise him on what they should be doing, 'and I used to feel, being a young man not long out of college where part of my studies had included brass band music, that I knew best.' He laughed. 'There were no hard feelings, though.' " '

'By bloody 'ell but there were,' burst in Stirling. 'I remember Horny's dad telling us how one night, after everybody had been complaining about his choice of music for a concert they were doing, Bernard asked them - he were always very polite, you know, 'Well, gentlemen, what would you like to see in front of you?' and t'bass trombone said, quick as you like, 'T'door of bandroom closing in mi rear view mirror!' '

Dolores laughed. 'It goes on to talk about when the band got in the National Finals.'

Stirling groaned. 'Bloody 'ell. Oh, no!' He shivered.

'Well, listen to what Bernard says about it. "It was one of the most wonderful days of my life. Like all the band I knew my wife was in the Albert Hall, and I wanted to play well for her, of course, because she's always been a great supporter of the band." '

Stirling sniggered.

Dolores said sharply 'Now I want no mucky suggestions from you. Lil's been a good friend to all - now then stop it! - all the band, players and supporters. Just shut up for once and listen to what Bernard had to say to this reporter lass.

" 'I wish I could bottle the experience and give the bottles to everyone whenever they feel low,' Bernard told me. 'Walking out on to that stage is awesome. The vast auditorium is like nowhere else in the world, so top-class players have told me. For me it seemed full of ghosts of the great players and conductors of the past. Then I was extremely proud of the band, that we'd worked so hard and got there, and let me tell your readers that it is a huge financial effort for a village band to collect the three thousand or so pounds needed for a band to compete in the National Finals.

'I don't think I can start to do justice to the supreme moment,' he said. 'Just the few seconds when I'd turned my back on the vast hall, and waited for silence, then lifted my arms to gather the band, knowing that this was the moment we'd worked so long for, let me tell you it made life worth living' ".'

Stirling was silent after Dolores stopped reading.

'You can work wi' somebody, and think you know them,' he began at last, 'an' you're so far wrong that you might as well have never bloody met 'em. No, it's not that. I suppose what it is, he's put things into words there that I never knew I felt. So maybe it's me that I've never known. Bloody 'ell, how can I explain? He talks about school, wi' happy memories, and I remember how Horny and me used to mek a fool of him. But the happy memories of school are true for me as well as Bernard. An' what he said then about t'Albert Hall, that were just right, but I never knew I felt it. Funny, eh?'

He sat for a long time, thinking, said, 'I'll just go an' see if Horny fancies a pint. All right, love?' then kissed her thoughtfully and went out of the room, closing the door with unusual gentleness.

Several of the regulars had read the article in the paper and it was the talk of the pub when Stirling and Horny got there.

'Hey, you two,' said Reg. "Ow well do you remember t'time we nearly won t'National?'

'Nay,' said Horny. 'There's a daft question. 'Who can forget an experience like that?'

The National

The last crashing chord rolled round St. George's Hall and then silence seemed to hang in the air interminably. Applause spattered. The audience was thin; nobody bothered to sit in the hall for Harden Moss.

'Might as well get a pint in. Back for Marsden,' they'd say as Harden Moss players were filing on to the stage. 'Good band, Marsden.'

But the players were swept to their feet by a strangely exultant conductor.

'Wonderful, gentlemen,' Bernard said. 'That was real playing. We'll win with that.'

'Nay,' murmured Horny to Stirling. 'He'd better be wrong there. We can't afford to win. That'd take us up to second section! 'How would we cope? We were designed as a third section band. We're right as a third section band.'

'Too bloody true,' growled Stirling as they ambled from the stage while the audience began to take their seats for Marsden. 'Now them lads'll bloody walk it! Poor sods. Then they'll 'ave to start scraping money together to get to London for National Finals. Poor bloody sods.'

The contest had just finished and St George's Hall was packed. Supporters for each of the third section bands in the area had clumped themselves together so that they could cheer their heroes when they won. Harden Moss heroes were in the bar. After all, as Tommy regularly said to the other two members of the trombone section, 'Why waste drinking time waiting for t'results? It's not a bad pint, after all.'

Bernard was with the women in the hall, waiting with a strange feeling in his heart. All through the dreary speechifying, and the listing of the sixth, fifth, fourth and third placed bands he was trying to identify the feeling. When the endless teasing of the chairman of the local association culminated in the announcement that ... 'In second place with 179 points: the band that played number 7, Harden Moss,' the cheer that went up was a powerful solo performance by Lil with, as backing group, the piping voices of young girlfriends still sufficiently in love to waste a precious Sunday listening to the same piece of music played with earnest effort by twenty two bands.

'We've won!' Lil gave Bernard a warm, proud kiss. 'That's wonderful.'

Bernard suddenly remembered what that waiting, half-breathing feeling in his heart was. Still he had a duty to truth.

'Not quite won,' he said pedantically. He was, after all, a school teacher in his spare time. 'But we will be going to London for the finals. It's good luck that the lower sections are going to compete in the Albert Hall again this year. I wonder how we'll be able to afford it.'

The downstairs bar was full of men who looked identical except for the colour of their uniforms, scarlet with gold braid, blue with gold braid, green with gold braid, even gold with gold braid, all backed with lion tamer stripes, each jacket of whatever colour gaping comfortably over a wide white-shirted belly, and each white shirt surmounted by a deep red face, a face alive with delight in banding and beer and good company. Stirling and Horny found themselves accosted.

'Hey up, lads; beer's on Harden Moss, to-neet, i'n't it?' and

' 'Ow does it feel to win?'

They felt faint, suddenly, and had to sit down and have a whisky each to regain the steadiness of their right elbows.

'Bloody 'ell. Just think of that, eh, Horny. Bloody 'ell!'

The next months were feverish. The band's clubroom bar was the centre of fund-raising activity. The three members of the trombone section were asked to contribute the same amount again every time they bought a pint.

'Should have the whole three thousand in a couple of weeks, then,' said Reg, the steady E flat bass player.

Reg and his property-owning bass section reluctantly agreed to set up a temporary endowment which would be tax-free, based on a tenth of the weekly rent of the properties they purchased with the proceeds of the band's pools win.

Bernard's mother, with a severely martyred air, was knitting egg cosies to be raffled.

From each according to his or her talent.

People associated with the band changed in those eight months.

Bernard, the solitary teacher at the Harden Moss Junior and Infants School, was different following the band's triumphant second placing. Tricia, his non-teaching assistant, a tiny, terrifying teenager and daughter of Tommy the bass trombone, noticed the difference. She found that she no longer had to enforce discipline in the school. It was as if Bernard had found new confidence.

Billy the euphonium player, once small himself, now a gangling six foot sixer and bent over as if perpetually avoiding low ceilings, seemed to grow even faster. Lil, who looked after uniforms, gave up trying to keep him in one that fitted.

'We'll keep some spare sleeve ends from worn-out jackets and tack 'em on where the gold braid starts,' she told him. 'It won't matter if you've got a double set of braid.'

Stirling and Horny started taking their instruments home to practise. Every evening after tea Stirling would go round to Horny's allotment shed, pungent with the smells of rotting garden tools, beer and brasso, and they would sit together and blow.

'I'm too bloody old for this,' Stirling would grumble. 'I'm goin' to wear me bloody teeth out at this rate. One of them's gettin' a bit shaky as it is.'

The set piece for the Third Section Finals had been commissioned from Alexander Smith and was called *Dykes and Braes*.

'It'll grow on you, gentlemen,' Bernard assured them after the first week's rehearsal. 'Try to imagine the heather-clad northern hills, glowing in the last light of a winter sun.'

'I'd rather imagine the soft light of the bar glowing through a malt whisky,' murmured Horny to Stirling. 'Hey,' practising a few notes, 'listen, it works!'

'It's bloody flugel solo in t'slow movement that's worrying me,' said Stirling. 'I can fair hear that bloody tooth of mine rattling when I'm glissandoing up to that top B flat.'

By the time that the jumble sales and cricket events and bring and buys and raffles and race nights had played their part so that the coach and the two nights in the London hotel could be booked it was late September. Only two weeks to go.

The band was rehearsing almost every night and the supporters were meeting regularly to plan the shows they would go to and the clothes they would wear.

'I'll be bloody glad when this nonsense is over and done wi',' said Stirling to Horny after a distressing rehearsal one night. 'Bernard isn't 'isself. He's that bloody keen that I've practically blowed the plating off mi mouthpiece, struggling to get it right for 'im. I'm not 'appy.'

'Think of all this fuss and bother as a two-bar cadenza in an overture of after-beats,' Horny said, then had the grace to blush when he saw Stirling's deliberate double take. 'What I mean is, at least it makes a change. I don't suppose Dolores is going, is she?'

'Funny you should ask. She bloody is! Fust time I can remember 'er going to a bloody contest. What'll we talk about all weekend?'

He needn't have worried. The weekend was strictly segregated, the players working, the women playing with London. If Bernard had had his way it would have been completely segregated in the belief that concentration is aided by sexual abstinence.

He would certainly have found it a help. Lil was a dominant woman who found excitement an aphrodisiac. What with school, where the children were relying more and more on teenager Tricia for genuine education, almost daily and extended rehearsals, and Lil warm and lustful when he got home, Bernard was exhausted. He was kept going only by the magnificence of the thought that he would soon be conducting on the stage where the great and good had stood before their musicians, Sir Henry Wood, Sir Malcolm Sargent ... In the dark, sleepless reaches of the night Bernard's brain would scenario the talent scout for the L.S.O. approaching Bernard after the contest, and, later, the acclaim for Sir Bernard when he visited his home village of Harden Moss.

Contest Day. Sunday. The Albert Hall was still warm from the glorious blowing of the Championship Section on the Saturday. The Third Section draw would be at noon and the bands would start playing at 2.30.

Horny and Stirling met at breakfast.

'Last rehearsal, then,' said Stirling as they walked back to their table carrying plates highly structured with sausages, hash browns, onion rings, mushrooms, baked beans, black-pudding, eggs and bacon. 'Bloody good job, too. Dolores got a bit passionate last night and ...'

'Oh, aye. Did she like the show?'

'Said it were bloody real. I should imagine she felt at home, don't you? Marsden Street in Harden Moss can't be all that bloody different from Sunset Boulevard in Hollywood. Anyway ... pass that tomato sauce, will you? You know 'ow quiet she is. Doesn't say a bloody word.'

'We've all always envied you.'

'Aye, well last night, when I wanted mi sleep and all, she wouldn't shut up. Wanted to tell me, ME! about the bloody dresses in the show! An' the only way to shut her up was ... well, what 'appened was ... Salt.'

'Stirling. Tell us.'

'Well, it's embarrassing. Let me show you!'

For a horrified moment Horny wondered what Stirling was going to reveal but what did emerge was even worse than he had been imagining. Stirling pulled back his top lip and pushed the tip of an eggy tongue through a large gap.

'There. Told you mi tooth was loose. Now how am I going to play mi solo?'

Four fifty eight. Harden Moss Band, drawn number ten, walked steadily on to the stage of the Royal Albert Hall. From the excellent seats in the balcony which the Harden Moss supporters had commandeered Lil looked anxiously to see if the joins showed on Billy's sleeves. No. Not from that distance anyway. She relaxed.

Instruments were shining, uniforms immaculate. Each man swept the circle of the auditorium with his eyes to establish home base before fixing his gaze within the semi-circle of the band. They stood, instruments embraced in strong Harden Moss right arms, waiting for Bernard. As he walked on to the stage there was a gentle rattle of applause with a focal point of cheering intensity from the band's supporters.

Each of the players, adrenalin exaggerating his senses, heard the voice of his own woman across the chasm of distance. Bernard remembered for a flash of a second his distant longing for Lil long ago. But this, here and now, this was the moment he had never allowed himself to dream of. He would not now have changed places with any man in the world. This was the great moment of his life. He lifted his arms, collected the attention of the twenty five men in front of him, held his position until the coughs and rustles from the hall had died, so that all that was behind him was a vast resounding hollow of emptiness and he was the emperor of the world, then raised his baton, gathered them again and they began.

Thirteen and a half minutes later, all hope gone, they turned to acknowledge the brave cheers of their supporters then with dignity walked off the stage.

'What can I bloody say?' said Stirling to Bernard. 'I lost it for us. It weren't just mi tooth and the super-glue on the bit I'd cut from the toothbrush. It were mi bottle that went. Bloody hell, Bernard. We shall never get here again, and I lost it for us.'

Bernard turned to face Stirling. If he'd been American he'd have put an arm around his shoulders and hugged him. As he was from Harden Moss he felt slightly embarrassed to look another man in the face and speak, but he managed it.

'Yes, we've lost, but we were here. Don't you see, Stirling? You and Horny and Billy and Tommy and Reg and Ticker and the rest, we've done a wonderful thing. You'll forget about your tooth, I hope, but you'll be able to tell your grandchildren that you played on the stage of the Royal Albert Hall. I'm proud of us all.'

Lil, Dolores and the other women were furious at the result.

'We were robbed,' said Lil. 'Them adjudicators didn't know what they were doing, putting us at next to the bottom. Never mind,

Bernard. You looked marvellous. We were so proud of you all. And Billy's jacket didn't matter at all.'

Dolores smiled at Stirling. 'Better than Sunset Boulevard,' she said.

The coach set off on its journey north at a quarter past midnight after an evening of furious revelry. Dolores fell asleep almost at once with a smile on her face, square head comfortably settled down onto square shoulders, and Stirling slipped into the empty seat beside Horny.

'No rehearsal on Tuesday,' he said. 'What'll us bloody do with ourselves?'

'Come over to our shed. I've bought the score for next year's area test piece. If we start rehearsing now we might just be able to do it all again. Eh, Stirling?'

The Garden Party

The ladies of the band had been invited to Lil's. She was holding a summer garden party to celebrate Bernard's retirement and she let it be known that she would appreciate help with the arrangements.

Dolores called for Annie and together they walked up the hill to the house which had been known as the school house since Bernard moved into it with his bride almost thirty years ago. It was a lovely day of late summer. If they had looked, Dolores and Annie would have noticed how dangerously sharp against the blue was the line of the hills.

They were carrying bags or baskets, because Lil had also let it be known to the ladies that a faith supper would be in order. Faith lay not in the dutifulness of the food bringers but in blind trust as to what the result would be. A faith supper at the local chapel had once resulted in sixteen plates of cakes, four of them orange cakes, two plates of rock cakes from the strictest believers and the other ten chocolate cakes in various degrees of lusciousness.

Annie and Dolores had consulted. Annie's spiced chicken legs would eat very well with Dolores' (M&S) rice salad. As they climbed slowly they talked. Since Annie had materialised in Horny's life over a year ago, she and Dolores had become good friends. Dolores was happier. Less of a loner.

They were talking about Lil and her mother-in-law.

'I well remember when Bernard brought Lil home from Amsterdam as his fiancée. I had my eye on Stirling then, so it was useful; it set up a kind of habit. The idea of getting wed didn't seem so bad to him when he could see Bernard was all for it. But you ought to have heard Bernard's mother. In fact you could have heard her all over the village! She went wild. Bernard actually cleared out of her house and slept on a put-u-up in the school until he and Lil got married and moved up the road here.'

'Did she accept Lil after the wedding?' asked Annie.

'Not easily. It was her loss. Bernard was that taken-up with Lil that he wouldn't really have noticed if the whole village, including all his school kids, had moved away. It was a schooling in love to watch him. He and Lil used to go to his mother's for tea on Sundays, and the word in the village was that Lil sat and talked, Bernard's mother sat and glared and Bernard sat and looked at Lil.'

'The old lady's coming today, I understand. She must be ninety or thereabouts. She lives in a home, doesn't she?'

'Yes. Still sits and knits. She must have knitted enough to go round the world three times. Still as bad-tempered as she ever was. And Dawn's coming too. Have you ever met her?'

'No. She's the daughter, isn't she? I well remember how Bernard put her into Horny's chair and Horny resigned from the band. Really. Men.'

Their men were standing in one corner of the garden.

'I 'ate do's,' said Stirling. 'Most any kind of bloody do. Weddings, Christmasses, they're all as bad, unless we're playin'.'

'Doesn't Lil look splendid?' said Horny appreciatively. 'I love her sense of danger. She'll wear things that other women know are in dreadful taste. Like that sort of souffle wrapped round her hips. What's it supposed to do for her? And how about the colours she's got on.'

'Not a soufflé, more of a luminous bloody Knickerbocker Glory,' said Stirling. 'Wi' t' wafer and t'cherry stuck on 'er 'ead. Hey up, t'bloody ambulance-taxi's 'ere. Must be Bernard's mum. Let's stroll up and see if we can't find another drink - and watch the fun.'

Bernard's mother emerged from the vehicle infinitely slowly, helped by the taxi driver, Bernard and Dawn, to collapse into the comfort of a wheelchair. Her tiny, black-clad figure almost disappeared into the cushions. Dawn tucked a large knitted rug over her knees. A cold sun was gradually withdrawing itself from the proceedings, regarding the party with distant contempt from behind thickening high cloud. Bernard's mother looked with similar coldness on the large, irridescent figure of Lil which was moving regally towards her.

As Lil bent to brush her cheek against the carefully combed white hair of her mother in law, she was bumped away by a boney skull as the old lady turned, whining wheezily, 'Our Bernard, get me a cup of tea, will you? Two sugars, in case you've forgotten. And a dry biscuit. If it's not too much trouble.'

'Won't you let me take you round the garden, to meet people, mother?' said Lil. 'There's ever so many people here you'll know.'

'I can see there's the lads who give our Bernard a bad stomach when he started teaching. If I'd had my way I'd have been in that classroom sorting them out. I told his headteacher, Mr Brown. Tried it on with me once, that Mr Fancy-pants Brown. I showed him what was what,' and the old lady cackled with laughter at the memory.

Horny and Stirling, at whom she'd been staring, shivered in unison.

'And there's that little square girl with the silly name. Not very bright,' she continued in a creaking, carrying voice. 'Not worn very well, either. And the drunken trombone player. Still trying to drink yourself to death, eh, you, whatsyourname?'

Horny, Stirling, Dolores and Tommy having been professionally stripped and their bones gnawed bare, Lil swung the chair back towards a part of the garden where there were fewer people whom Bernard's mother might know. The cloud had thickened now and the sky looked the consistency of old green lentil soup.

'Hey, lad, there's going to be bloody watter in this beer and it's none too strong to start with. D'you think we can escape soon?' said Stirling longingly.

As he spoke the waterfall began to pour from the sky.

The garden, which sloped steadily from the house down to a low stone wall, offered a perfect river bed for the water which was looking for a home.

Lil, trying to pull her mother-in-law's wheelchair back up the path to the shelter of the house, slipped, lost her grip of the handles and landed on her souffle. The escaping wheelchair bumped and ground its way across a flower-bed, down a small lawn and was obviously aiming to hit the wall at a perfect angle to catapult Bernard's mother up and out over the valley below.

Everyone ran to reach the racing chair.

Horny and Stirling were nearest. They slipped, skidded, leaped and took giant strides. They could see Bernard's mother's head woggling like a toy dog in the rear window of an ancient Anglia driven by a man in a cap.

Horny was first to reach the chair. His hand slipped off the handle as it started to tilt forward. Stirling flung himself full length into the chair, knocking it on to its side and Horny caught its weight before it hit the ground.

Stirling picked himself up off his knees. He touched the blood which was joining the rain running down his forehead and looked at Horny who was turning the wheelchair back towards the house, limping from a twisted knee.

Bernard's mother swivelled her head and snapped a glance at each of them.

'You look as if you've been in the wars,' she wheezed. 'Serves you right. You were always naughty boys. Got your comeuppance now, eh? Heh, heh, heh.'

The heroes were relieved of their cantankerous burden and fresh glasses foaming with widget-rich ale were pressed into their hands. Then to their relief they were forgotten and leaned peacefully alongside Tommy and Reg against a wall in a quiet passage somewhere in the house.

'We've leaned against a few walls and supped a few pints in us time,' said Reg.

'Aye,' said the other three then said nothing for several minutes.

'Ah'm fair glad old Bernard is sticking wi' band. What would the daft old sod 'ave 'ad in 'is life if 'e'd left that as well as t'school?'

'Aye,' the others said again.

'This beer's pretty fair,' said Horny.

'Well, let's get us-selves another can before it's all wasted on them as doesn't appreciate a decent bloody pint,' said Stirling and the four of them drifted companionably back to the school house kitchen to search for four more cans of acceptable beer.

'This is turning into a reasonable party,' said Horny to Stirling as they regained their bit of wall.

'Aye,' said Stirling.

The Wedding

'It's raining again. Let me come in and get dry,' said Annie, opening the front door as she spoke. 'What a horrible evening.'

'I was really glad to see the back of our Stirling tonight. He was so grumpy. Not a nice word out of him. Not that that's unusual,' said Dolores, leading her visitor through into the warmth of the living room. 'Sit down. D'you fancy a coffee or something more cheerful?'

Annie fished in the carrier she'd brought with her which had clunked promisingly when she put it down on the carpet beside her chair.

'Well, I thought we could have a go at this, when you've heard my news.' She pulled out a heavy green bottle with a glinting gold foil top. 'It's real. Not one of your sparkling whites.'

Dolores's eyes lit up but she only said, 'I'll put it in the fridge, shall I? Till you've told me.'

Annie waited, smiling, till she came back and sat down in the armchair opposite.

'You're good at waiting, aren't you? No nattering. Patience, eh?'

'No, just Stirling. It's an education in patience, being married … to him.'

On the word 'married' Dolores's voice faltered. She looked across at Annie. Annie smiled then began to chuckle then to laugh. After a moment Dolores joined in and the two women rocked in their chairs.

Annie recovered first and lay back, wiping her eyes with her hand.

'Your face was a picture, Dolores. Why are you so surprised? We've lived together for well over a year, now.'

'Yes. That's true. It's just that you and Horny have seemed so easy, somehow, since you moved in with him, and it's all felt right. Comfortable. It's almost an upset to think of you going conventional and getting wed. Not that I'm not delighted, mind. Horny's closer to Stir than his own brother could have been, and I used to fair worry about him, all those years when he seemed to be gathering no worthwhile moss, either the jobs or lasses sort.'

She got up impulsively and went over to Annie's chair and gave her a brief and awkward hug.

'I'm very glad, Annie. It'll fix you here for good. Not that I ever doubted that you'd stay.' She stood, her face shining, looking complacently at her friend. 'Tell me why you decided when I've brought the champagne back and you've opened it.'

Ordinary wine glasses frilled with bubbles as fizzily as flutes would have done, and Dolores and Annie clinked and drank then sat looking contentedly at each other.

'Go on, then,' said Dolores.

'I think it goes back to what you just said, that Horny had started to feel that the only sure things in his life were this village and Stir and the band, before he met me, that is. Now he wants to tie everything up in one package. And I don't mean only him and me, I mean Harden Moss and you two and the band. He's decided that he's found out what life's about ...'

Dolores interrupted. 'He's always been a thinker, Stir says.'

'And for him it's happiness. Here. So we're going to go to the registry office in Huddersfield and we'd like you two to come with us as our witnesses. My brother will come too, but he's the only family we've got between us.'

Dolores's bright face fell. 'Surely you're going to have a party. And the band playing for you. The church down in the village is really pretty for a wedding.'

'No. We'll do the deed, but Horny's not a great one for parties and noise. And we're not church goers. Here, have a refill.'

A vaguely similar scene was being played in the pub. Stirling was just going to the bar to buy his round when Horny said, 'Um, Stirling.' Then stopped.

Stirling waited, then after a moment or two of silence stopped waiting and set off for the drinks.

When he'd put the glasses down carefully on the table between them Horny tried again.

'It's me and Annie,' he began, and stopped for a second time.

Stirling ignored him for a second time and took a long, comfortable drink.

'This is the best bloody beer Gabby's had on since … ooh … last February. Remember when we'd just played at the area and we came in here to drown us sorrows and …'

'Annie and me, we've decided to get wed.'

'and Gabby gave us fust bloody pints free because … he was so … What did you say?'

'Wed,' said Horny, his head down.

Stirling looked at the top of Horny's head. His hair was thinning fast, he noticed.

'Stress,' he said.

'What?'

'Th'art going bald. It comes from living too close to another person, specially a lass.' He drank half his pint thoughtfully. 'And you tell me you're going to tie a bloody knot, you and Annie?' He drained his glass. 'Well, I've always thought Annie was lovely and too bloody good for thee. So I reckon I'm chuffed that you've nabbed her before she saw the bloody error of her ways and escaped.'

He stuck his hand across the table. Horny shook it.

'What are we going to play?'

'No.'

' 'Aven't you decided? I allus think that *Love Divine* goes down a treat. Played a bit slow, like. It's your round.'

'No, Stir.' Horny said. 'We're not having a proper do. No band. I want it quiet. Annie's at your house now asking Dolores if you and she will come as our witnesses. And we'll go for an Indian after. Only the four of us and Annie's brother.'

Stirling was sitting as though he'd been turned to stone. He could have been taken for an ugly modern statue called 'Shock'.

He hadn't moved by the time Horny got back to the table with their new pints. Horny passed his hand solemnly in front of Stirling's eyes. 'When you awaken from this trance you will be a new man,' he intoned. 'You will forswear swearing and never again let strong liquor touch your lips.'

'Bloody 'ell, that took me by surprise.' Stirling automatically put out his hand and took hold of his glass. 'I don't just need a pint, I need a whisky.' And as he drank his eyes looked over his glass as if into vasty distances, like an explorer gazing into a strange new world.

Saturday the eleventh was grey and cool. But it was at least dry, which Dolores said she was pleased about as she gave Stirling a weather report over breakfast.

'My new red suit will look really cheerful without my mac. I've chosen one of your ties that has just the same red, so we'll match.'

Stirling growled a comment which Dolores didn't ask him to repeat. But he did, anyway.

'I said bugger the weather. And I'm buggered if I want us to look like Jack and bloody Jill, a dreadful warning to any hopefuls in t'registry office.'

'Annie's got a lovely pink outfit, and she was wondering about dying her hair to tone with it.'

'Is Horny wearing pink too? Another matching bloody pair? Should suit 'im. Any man 'oo puts 'is 'ead into this bloody marriage noose needs dressing up like an organ grinder's monkey. He's got no more sense.'

'Hmmm.' Dolores looked sideways at him as she got up and cleared the table. 'A fine mess you'd be in without me. Why, you wouldn't even know where I put your shirts!'

'If I hadn't got you you wouldn't 'ave put the bloody things anywh ... Oh, what's the use. Trying to talk to a woman is like peeing over the wrong side of a boat in a high wind.'

Three houses away Horny and Annie were arguing.

'Why are we arguing? We never argue. We've not argued in over a year of living here. Maybe it's because we're getting married. D'you think we should call it off?' asked Horny of Annie's back as she leant over the bath trying to wash the dye out of her hair.

'You've washed your hair eight times now, or is it nine? Any road, the hair can't defy you much longer. It must know when it isn't wanted. It'll give up trying to please you soon and I shall be taking a bald woman to the office altar.'

'You should know when you aren't wanted, which is now,' flashed Annie, swinging round and flinging pink droplets of water over Horny's crisp white shirt. 'Shit. Now you'll look like what was his name … that great fat chap. And I don't think you've got another clean shirt. Shit.'

Horny put his arms round her cross wet back and hugged her.

'I'm totally, utterly happy for the first time in my life. I can't wait to be able to call you my wife, even if I have to say I, Mister Blobby, take you, Annie, for better for worse. There'll be no worse, so far as I'm concerned.'

Huddersfield town centre was its usual active Saturday self while the registry office carried on the quiet business of life and death unobtrusively under the noses of shoppers and the police at their station. Five gaudily dressed people, or rather, two gaudily dressed women and three men ornamented with matching flashes of gaudiness hung around on the steps outside, waiting for the previous couple to be showered with confetti and move on into normal life, leaving them to complete their own entry in the register of officialdom.

'They're nodding to us. Get a bloody move on, lad,' said Stirling, looking up the street as Dolores, leaning heavily on his arm, plonked in her high heels down the steps and towards the office doors.

The ceremony was thoughtful, solemn and honest, asking for the same virtues from the people asking to be wed.

This is all lovely, thought Stirling, deeply moved. He watched his lifetime's friend, Horny the uncommitted, vowing constancy and total commitment to the bright woman with pink hair beside him. He means it, all of it, thought Stirling. I wonder how much I meant when I married our Dolores. He looked sideways at her out of the corner of his eye and patted her hand which lay on her knee, holding a hankie, in case. She looked up at him and smiled and shuffled an inch closer.

It's been all right, on the whole, I suppose, Stirling's thoughts continued.

I wonder whether to have chicken or lamb balti for dinner.

His thoughts meandered on through happy reminiscences of previous curries then suddenly he was being asked to sign as Horny's witness.

'It's a bit like being a guarantor for a debt,' Horny told him. 'If I default, the liability for this marriage becomes yours.'

'Can't think of owt I'd like bl ... better,' Stirling said with polished charm and he wrote his signature slowly, neatly, carefully.

Daylight seemed to have brightened as they approached the swing doors to leave then suddenly the brightness was full of snow, multi-coloured snow. Immediately in front of the notices which said loudly NO CONFETTI all the members of the junior band were crouching, armed with great handfuls of the stuff which they fired as the air began to ring with *Love Divine*.

The band, grand in caps and green and gold dress uniforms, loomed above the junior band on the steps outside the registry office. The bell of every instrument was trained on the happy couple and their witnesses, and the sound was awesome.

'Shock an' bloody awe,' Stirling leaned forwards to murmur into Horny's ear. 'And the right sort.'

The band played their magnificent nuptial way through the streets of Huddersfield, with Horny and Annie forced to lead the procession.

The streets gradually filled with appreciative onlookers, particularly men who found the noise a welcome relief from questions such as 'Does this suit me better than the slinky one? Or did you prefer the trousers?'

Annie's embarrassed red face clashed violently with her pink outfit and hair but she clutched Horny's hand and strode out bravely, Dolores kicked off her shoes and carried them, walking in the middle of the parade beside Tim the timps, while Stirling, whose flugel had been warmed up for him by the first horn player, and Annie's brother, who had arranged for someone to bring a spare cornet, hid within the green-uniformed bulk of the band.

The lyres held a short selection of what Stirling liked best for weddings, plus *Hail, Smiling Morn*, which he just liked. They had set off, as they left the registry office with its collection of scandalised but amused officials, in the magnificence of Wagner's *Wedding March from Lohengrin*. This took them down to the Town Hall. *Love Divine* was called on again here, then they hailed their own particular smiling morn before they reached Queen Street.

Bernard halted the traffic, feeling like his old headmastery self, and they marched spectacularly across in front of the waiting traffic playing *Annie Laurie*. Annie managed to blush even more, with crowds of appreciative kids skipping along beside.

'Will you play at my wedding, mister?' Bernard was asked by a dirty small girl.

A vigorous burst of *Congratulations* took them to the door of Mem Sahib, their chosen restaurant, which had been booked in its entirety by Stirling. The wives and girlfriends waiting there cheered the happy couple as the band filled the restaurant, but their voices were soon drowned as the bandsmen found that they couldn't stop playing and reprised the entire programme.

'By bloody 'ell but that were good,' said Stirling to Horny as he handed him his first pint of Kingfisher. 'I bet tha's glad tha didn't 'ave such a quiet wedding as tha'd planned. A bloody sight better this way,' he added firmly.

He leaned across Horny to Annie.

'And the Examiner'll 'ave it all over its front page tonight. I saw the photographer just as you and your husband here led us all past t'Town Hall.'

The waiter was hovering.

'Right, lad,' continued Stirling. 'I'll 'ave your special, lamb and chicken and prawn balti. And rice. And a keema nan. I'm bloody starving.'

'Stir,' said Horny.

Stirling jumped in over-exaggerated surprise. 'I'd assumed tha'd tekken a vow of silence along wi' t'other vow. Fust time tha's spoke since tha got wed.'

'Stir,' Horny said again. 'I want you to know that I'm likely going to be using that office again. Soon.'

'Nay, congratulations surely aren't in order yet, are they? Bloody 'ell. Tha'rt a fast worker.'

'No, Stirling. Three functions, hasn't it? Hatching, matching and what's the other? It's slipped me mind for the moment, but … oh, yes, I've got it, the one that fits thee.'

He paused, weightily.

'Despatching.' said Horny darkly.

A Bandsman's Year

'Are you into t'W.I.?' Stirling asked Horny one November rehearsal, between pieces.

'What? What are you on about? What is it Bernard's told us to look for in our pads? '

'*Endearing Young Charms*. Fits pretty well wi' Women's Institute, when you consider. Must've been what reminded me.'

'Are we all ready?' asked Bernard. 'If I may interrupt your conversation, flugel and horn. One, two ...'

The melody sang its sweet nostalgic song and Widget played his delicate solo part.

'That's just 'ow we should mek it,' said Stirling as they put their instruments on their knees and rummaged in their pads for *Trumpets A-Go-Go*. 'Delicate. Innocent.'

'What are you on about?' asked Horny again. 'Who's got to be delicate and innocent?'

'Us, of course,' Stirling hissed from behind his hand. Bernard was looking cross.

'Stirling, you've lost it. Whatever are you rambling on about?'

'Tell you after.'

Trumpets went, in their own time, and during the short break which followed Stirling again approached the subject which was clearly close to his heart.

'With bits of us bloody instruments in't way, you know.'

Horny exploded. 'In the way of what? What mad idea have you got in that thick skull? Your plumbing system leaks, Stir.'

'I told thee. Like that W.I. calendar. Instruments in front of us own bloody plumbing systems. You're allus goin' on about us mekking money, well, this'll get us a fortune. Millions. Don't you think it's a bloody good idea?'

'Am I getting close? Are you suggesting we take our clothes off, Stirling? You, and Bernard, and young Alexander? And old Reg? And me? '

'Well, that shouldn't bother thee too much. Half the bloody population of Harden Moss have seen thee stark bollock naked. Or so I am led to believe.' Stirling picked up his instrument and blew thoughtfully into his mouthpiece. 'The female half, that is.'

He leaned over just as Horny was about to play and hissed, 'I can picture this production wi' a song title and a few bars of music under each photo. You could 'ave *Swing Low* under thine.'

In the bar, after the rehearsal and the first refreshing pints, Horny pulled a piece of paper out of his pocket, found a pen that worked and put both alongside his pint glass.

'Right,' he said. 'I think that Tommy and his team should have *The Blades of Toledo* under their picture and they should be doing a kind of song and dance act with their slides positioned just so.'

'So you think it's a bloody good idea, eh? Right, then. 'Ave you ever seen old Reg wi'out his bloody kegs? 'E's got to 'ave *How Great Thou Art* for 'is tune.'

Widget pulled up a chair to their table. They explained their plan and his face lit up. 'Brilliant idea, Stir. We'll collect a list of pieces to fit all on us. For you, what about *Boom Bang-A-Bang?*'

'Nay, that'd do better for poor old Tim the timps,' said Horny. 'We should have *The Stripper* for Stirling, in tribute to Dolores.'

'Or *Jingle Bells,*' said Tommy, joining in. '*And Hey Look Me Over* would be nice for Horny. Reminiscent, like.'

The session went well. By the time the pub shut, the team had decided important things, like how to insult each bandsman as completely as possible by the choice of the piece of music to go under his photograph. Widget even made a list. Alexander, since he was at school more recently than most of the others, was pressurised to start working on a second and more serious list, of how each month would be best represented. The tricky bit was combining the two.

'You know,' said Stirling to Horny as they were walking home. Late. 'Lil won't let this 'appen without 'er getting closely bloody involved. If you see what I mean.'

'No,' said Horny. 'Tell us.'

'Well, you remember we chose old Bernard to be January. Because 'e's got white 'air and, well, January is cold and bloody boring. Like … Well, we all understood that. And we 'ad a bit of fun over how 'e's going to cover 'is personal plumbing with 'is baton.'

Horny started laughing. 'So? Where does Lil come in?'

'And you know we talked about getting that bloody gorgeous photographer from t'Examiner to take pictures on us all?'

'Oh, I see. No way is Lil going to want Bernard to pose behind his baton for young Beatie the Beauty.'

'I can see Lil now, enrolling at photography evening class, then prancing around wi' 'er own Box bloody Brownie.'

They laughed all the way home, and were still happy enough when they got into their own houses to go on talking about the scheme.

Stirling explained to a sleepy Dolores, who said, 'Daft idea. Would be you thought of that, Stir. Daft. Mind you it'll be interesting to see …'

At about the same time Horny was telling Annie who sat up in bed, wide-eyed with excitement. 'That'll be brilliant. Will you get the Examiner to market it? With the band and the paper sharing profits? You need a committee, that's certain. Can I be on it, do you think, or haven't I lived here long enough?'

Harden Moss villagers buzzed as secretively as they possibly could.

'Wouldn't do to let Holme Silver or Hade Edge get wind of this or they'd be doing it themselves,' the members of the band and their supporters said to each other.

In early December the band interviewed Beautiful Beatrice of the Examiner.

She wore a flimsy floaty midriff-baring top and hipster jeans so tight that the eyes of many of the band, particularly the older ones, watered sympathetically. She charmed them all and flattered them and offered them the world, or that was the way it felt. In fact she offered them five percent of sales up to three thousand calendars and seven and a half per cent thereafter. The Examiner would cover all costs.

And she would take the pictures, if they would be agreeable.

The band purred and offered to buy her a pint. Each.

Harden Moss's world was pink and sweet, then Lil heard about the arrangement.

'What do you mean, Bernard?' she snapped when Bernard happened to mention that final detail, that Beatie would be the photographer. 'Amn't I good enough for you? After all these years. You used to think the snaps I took of us all were lovely,' and she dissolved into artistic tears. 'Can we not 'ave a committee?'

The committee of wives plus a gentle, smiling representative of Mossie's Garden Centre, the band sponsors, vetted all the music choices suggested by the band's own committee which consisted of the whole band. *Resurgam*, put forward as a supremely appropriate piece for Easter, particularly if played by Horny, was quashed as blasphemous, particularly if played by Horny. The band committee in its turn quashed such plans as having Widget's three little girls standing in pretty long dresses, crowned with coronets of spring flowers and with their arms entwined around his neck as he played *Believe Me If All Those Endearing Young Charms*. For May.

'Bloody 'ell,' said Stirling. 'I never thought it would get this nasty. There's Lil threatening to stop Bernard being in t'Calendar at all! And Reg threatening to pull out if 'e can't be playing Tubby the Tuba. Mind you, 'e's right. Shape fits 'im to an O.'

'How do you mean, to an O?' asked Widget. 'Oh, I see. A 'T' wouldn't fit him at all, would it?'

'Ain't there owt we're all agreed on besides us trombones playing *Blades of Toledo*?' asked Tommy. 'Hey. 'Ow do we manage wi' that?'

'You asking about the plumbing problem? Ask our resident plumber.'

'Don't be bloody simple, Tommy. You, as solo trom, stand wi' fust trombone bell end across yer ...'

'Bell end,' interrupted one of the back row cornets.

'... then second bell end across 'is, then ...'

'Then you've got a problem,' said Horny.

'We can allus ask Beatie to sort it out,' suggested Tommy.

'That might just increase the problem,' said Horny. 'Do something boring like putting a music stand in the way.'

'Or stand the bass trombone behind a tasteful Spanish-type statuette,' added the back row cornet.

'I thought we could balance on one leg each, a bit like Spanish dancers,' said Tommy's first trombone, 'but no doubt Beatie will ...'

'Sort it out,' the others chorused.

She sorted out a great deal.

'Should be on bloody conciliation thingy, that ACAS, she should,' said Stirling with admiration. ' 'Oo would've thought she'd mek us all agree to do January 'er way, whatever way that is, without telling us owt.'

'Or December,' said Horny.

'Young Tim's agreed. 'E don't look bad as she made 'im sit, wi' one of 'is timp sticks raised and t'other strategic, like,' said Reg. 'I'd never 'ave thought Tim would join in. Not ever. She's got to 'ave magic powers.'

After the heady excitement of deciding to make the Calendar, planning who would play what piece of music and for which month, the actual taking of the photographs might have been dull had not Beatie been the photographer.

Preparations and negotiations had occupied almost six months. The photos should be a doddle, the band thought. With Beatie in charge. Generally the work had to be done at weekends, and as the majority of the pictures were to be taken in the open air the temperamental Pennine weather had to be coaxed and cajoled into kindness. Beatie would manage it. She was imaginative in her use of natural backcloths. She had been born in the area and her family had moved away in her early teens, so she loved the valleys and moorland with the passion of someone who had been banished and returned.

They began filming in early summer and they planned that the photographs for the Calendar would be taken throughout June and July so that the whole thing could be ready in time for the Christmas avalanche of interest. Winter months' pictures could be mocked up easily, Beatie assured them. Choose the right summer setting, she said, and you should be able to make the picture convincing and strip with no discomfort.

Several of the bandsmen looked at her and groaned silently.

May was easy. Spring flowers surrounded the solo figure of Widget, leaning wistfully on a bank on which the wild thyme might well have blown, lyrically prim with artistic trails of artificial violets and primroses and forget-me-nots.

Josie was just off shot, monitoring. So were senior members of the band.

' 'Oo were that fairy woman, Horny? The one in't play. Lass 'oo falls for a donkey,' asked Stirling loudly. 'Our Widget looks like 'er.'

'You wait, Stir,' Widget hissed, trying to keep the hint of a smile on his lips as he mimed *Believe Me*.

A sunny day in June saw a fully clad Stirling walking with his flugel among young ash trees.

'That's so right,' said Beatie enthusiastically. 'You look wonderful, Stirling. Now let's get down to the nitty gritty, shall we?'

'Never heard it called that before,' growled Horny.

A flowery meadow was filled with the non-soloing members of the band crutch deep in long grass and buttercups to surmount a few bars from, inevitably, *Bells Across the Meadow* for July's page.

Horny looked modestly out above his own arrangement of *Annie's Song*, sitting on a rock in the bubbling and concealing water of the baby River Holme for August.

The trombones performed for September, Reg personified *Tubby the Tuba* for October, Tim was shoved with his timps into a disused quarry to represent November, all these being shot in a July which continued to be as sunny as June.

The Calendar had begun to develop a momentum of its own. Many of the wives, of course, followed Josie's example and refused to leave their naked men to be snapped by Beatie without the harsh eye of a wife overseeing. Interested villagers joined in.

'Let's try to get a good picture for *Night on a Bare Mountain* while the weather holds, guys,' said Beatie as they assembled in the centre of Harden Moss.

'Tough, that. Isn't it going to be played by back row cornets? What hope is there of owt good, then?' Horny said to Stirling as they drove in Stirling's old car, part of the cavalcade of vehicles which constituted the performers, film crew - Beatie with her cameras - and hangers-on.

Beatie had searched out the ideal place, she told them.

'Now, if we all leave our cars here in the picnic spot and walk … oh, you'll carry my gear, Reg? Thanks so much … You're all so sweet to me,' she threw over her shoulder as she trekked ahead of them up a narrow path, the members of the band who were in the cavalcade jostling to get into position immediately behind her.

'I'm fading away, wi' all this charging up and down t'bloody Pennines,' grumbled Stirling as he puffed up the track, last. 'I'm only supporting t'Calendar team because t'Yorkshire cricket team's so bloody rubbish.' He puffed some more, then called to Horny's disappearing rear, 'Nowt better to do on a Sat'day? Why's thy Annie here, anyroad?'

Horny stopped and waited for him, sighing in a fashion designed to annoy.

'Beatie's asked her if she'll help with the last three months' shots. Christmas is easy for the December page. All of us, walking down the street with nothing on but Father Christmas hats. Above *Jingle Bells*. I think they're going to film it early next Sunday morning before anybody's up. Annie's in charge of the costumes.'

'Huh. Costumes! And fat bloody chance there'll be nobody to watch. T'whole village will be out, laughing and bloody pointing.'

'*Swing Low* will be easy for March. Beatie wants the euphoniums to be walking along the far bank of the dam up at Yateholme while she films from the other side. Like looking over Jordan, she said. Annie understands that she's wondering about blurring the image just a little to protect their reputations. Nowt more.'

'What more do us bloody euphoniums need? Just a little bit of a blur. Will that be it, then? All done? Sit down 'ere for a minute so I can get me bloody breath back.'

'There's Bernard's big turn still. How Lil's going to like it I don't know. Annie says she's been trying to get in on the act but Beatie won't let her. As a professional.'

'*Winter Wonderland*, eh? White haired old Bernard wi' t'whole bloody band in t'snow. Where's Beatie wanting us to set up?'

'Apparently, according to Annie, we're going to do it straight after our Christmas number.'

'And the snow?'

'Annie said to wait and see. Oh, look, Stir. They must've finished. They're coming back down the track. They're going to trample on you. Shift.'

The following Sunday morning at four a.m. was as Stirling predicted. The whole village seemed to have turned out for the spectacle and to see the fine new Christmas decorations and brilliant festive lights, loaned by Kirklees on the warranty of The Examiner, shining on the polished instruments of their band.

'They should 'ave loud-speakered a bloody warning notice. Not suitable for them of a nervous disposition,' said Stirling to Horny as with one hand he tried to adjust the position of his own very personal Christmas decoration, dangerously concealed by a bunch of holly with artificial berries, while pulling his Father Christmas hat down over his face with the other.

'See that bus, there, at the end of the street? It's ready to take us to the winter wonderland. I have a horrible feeling that Beatie and Annie must have agreed that we leave us clothes in the bandroom, to save time.'

'And there's Lil,' said Stirling with horror in his voice, 'waiting ready at the foot of t'bus steps for us twenty bloody five or so naked men. Like a story I once read in a book called Hollywood Babylon.'

Bernard was waiting in the bus, since he had not been needed for the mock-up of the Christmas walk through the streets of Harden

Moss for December's picture. He was wearing vivid shorts and a lively shirt.

'Err...good morning, gentlemen,' he said in a quavering imitation of his usual voice as Stirling and Horny climbed on to the bus, past Lil. 'Err … ready, I see,' with a dangerously upward intonation, 'and perhaps as nervous as I.'

'Stirling, he could cop out,' said Horny as he sat down, winced and stood again before lowering himself gingerly on to the prickly plush seat. 'You don't think he's going to suggest that Lil takes his place in the Calendar, do you? She'd be glad to.'

With the whole band on board, and waving, the bus roared triumphantly past crowds of cheering villagers and up the hill towards the winter wonderland selected by Beatie with help from Annie.

'Annie didn't get home till very late last night. She told me yesterday that she'd not be able to. Over-seeing the decorations, and the Christmas lights, then the next bit.'

'What?'

'She wouldn't say. Wait and see, were what she said exactly.'

'Hey up, we're stopping. Horny, look where we are. Back door of Mossie's bloody Garden Centre.'

The door opened as the bus drew up and twenty five nervously shivering men slunk or strode or leapt or sidled through, according to temperament. Lil was at the door, handing out nondescript underpants which twenty five relieved men pulled on.

'Never thought Ah'd be so glad to see a pair of plain white knickers … on me, anyroad,' said Tommy as he leaned against a wall and struggled with a pair labelled Medium.

Tim's came up to his armpits.

'Swop,' said Tommy.

'There's no way these are c-c-coming off till I c-c-can see mine,' said Tim.

'Through here, lads,' purred Lil, patting them through a door.

Horny and Stirling threw an apprehensive glance at each other and followed the line. They found themselves in a band-sized semi-circle of chairs, with Harden Moss banners on the music stands.

'Home,' said Stirling.

They moved to their familiar places and found familiar instruments on their seats.

'Annie,' breathed Horny.

Each bandsman picked up his own instrument and put it automatically to his lips.

'Look!' said Stirling.

A snowy winter landscape was enclosing the stage in front of them, a very convincing landscape photographed on the hills above Harden Moss.

Stirling shivered. 'Too bloody real, that.'

'Are you ready, Bernard?' called Beatie's clear, bossy voice from behind them, and Bernard moved into his own familiar place. He stood behind his music stand. He took off his shirt and pushed his fingers through his white hair.

'I never thought we'd see our teacher wi'out a shirt,' said Horny.

'Will that do?' he called, pleadingly.

'Sorry, Bernard, darling,' Beatie answered. 'Shorts, please.'

'Or wi'out 'is bloody pants. What a sight, Horny. What does he look like? 'E reminds me of one of them luminous skellingtons you get painted on tee-shirts …'

'Or an expensive white painted bit of tree in IKEA you can hang baubles on for Christmas.'

Bernard's arms bravely raised, like bleached twigs waiting to be decorated, all instruments at lips, and eight flashes from Beatie's cameras later, the winter landscape suddenly cracked down the middle, and was folded and swept to the sides of the stage.

'Bloody 'ell,' said Stirling.

In front of them was a hall packed with people, laughing, applauding, cheering.

Bernard moved faster than light. The shorts and shirt leapt on. Annie was there at the front of the stage.

'Music pads are under seats,' she called. 'The Calendar programme! The music's in the right order!"

*   *   *   *

'So all those people had paid in advance, and paid well. They'll get their copies of the Calendar as soon as it's published, signed by every member of the band. I think they're on to a good thing. It'll be a collector's item,' Annie told them later.

'So 'oo'd 'ave paid for hospital bills if we'd all 'ad heart attacks?' asked Stirling. 'Specially Bernard. I swear them bloody shorts jumped on 'im themselves.'

'We played well enough, considering,' said Horny. 'Not a bad programme. Mind, there was no way in the world the soloists were going to stand up.'

'And I can't wait to see the Calendar, can you Annie?' said Dolores. 'Our own Calendar Boys, eh?'

Birthdays

The years were moving gently on in Harden Moss. Nothing seemed to change or get noticeably older.

'Annie,' called Dolores. 'Come and shelter in here. There's something I want to ask you.'

Dolores was standing in the doorway of the butcher's shop at the end of Battye Street, protecting her new hair-do from a squally wet wind which was sweeping winter in to Harden Moss.

'Phew, what a wind. End of autumn, don't you think? Now then, what did you want to tell me?'

'Not tell you so much as discuss. It's our Stirling's birthday in three weeks, and I know it's Horny's only a few weeks later. Both fifty. Can't believe it, can you?'

'And you reckon we should have a party? Brilliant idea,' said Annie, dark eyes sparking with excitement.

'Yes, and I think it should be in the band room. After all, banding's been the best part of Stirling's life, anyway, even if your Horny has managed to lift his mind to other things now and then. I wondered whether we could use the Harvest Festival night, if the band committee agrees.'

The annual auction, accompanied by pies, peas and playing, raised money for band funds by selling the goods, which bandsmen and their families brought, straight back to them at ridiculous prices.

'Anyway, the rain's easing off a little. Come home with me and have a cup of tea and we can talk it over.'

'What's this committee meeting for?' grumbled Widget to his second man at rehearsal that Thursday. 'I understand it's summat to do wi' the women. How come?'

'I'm never told,' said his second man who had even less personality than Tim.

'Right, lads,' began Tommy. 'I've called this special committee meeting, under powers vested in me ...'

'Oh, get on with it,' chorused the band in close harmony.

'... to discuss a proposal put to me by Stirling's wife ...'

'Get on with it,' double forte this time.

'Since Stir and Horny are fifty in a week or two, she and Annie hoped we could give them a do, like, at t'Harvest festivity.' Tommy sat down, disgruntled.

'That's why them two aren't here,' said Widget, with the air of the Prime Minister suddenly realising why his chancellor was raising tax on car fuel.

'Err... they had a prior engagement. With their wives,' said Bernard. He was deeply uneasy. He was approaching sixty five and he could not rid himself of the suspicion that Lil was planning a surprise party for him. He had told her repeatedly that he would far rather die, but he had a recurrent nightmare in which a stripper, dressed as a schools' inspector, would thoroughly and noisily Ofsted him in front of all his life's acquaintances.

'So what're we here for? Are we planning t'band's programme?' asked Tommy. 'We ought to play summat right for the pair of 'em. After all, they were practically founder members of t'present band.'

A chorus of ideas sang out.

'Hang on, we ought to 'ave a theme?' suggested Widget. 'Horny's easy. We just get all the songs written about women...'

'Aye, starting with *Lily of Laguna*. ...' said a back row cornet, then clapped his hand over his mouth as everyone turned to glare at him and a flush rose up Bernard's old neck.

'Well, yes, and Tommy, you could get a list together of some of his old flames. Stir's harder. He's been a great bandsman all his life. No other interest. Never really wandered far from t'village. And 'e's only ever been a plumber. Any music written about plumbers?'

The Harvest Festival started as it always did with a short concert by the band, just to get everyone comfortably settled, drinks in hand, and in cheery expectation of spending far too much.

'Daft bloody job this,' grumbled Stirling to Horny as they pulled up after cantering along with the *Washington Greys*. 'Why dun't everybody hand over twenty quid to them bloody highwaymen who run t'band funds wi'out all this fuss?'

'Dolores looks nice tonight,' answered Horny. 'Is that a new dress?'

'Bloody 'ell,' said Stirling looking at her. 'Bloody might be. When did she get that then?'

Bernard glared at them both as he raised his baton for *Just The Way You Look Tonight*.

The auction was unusual. All the commonplace tins of biscuits and soft toys had been replaced with wrapped gifts for Horny and Stirling. Annie and Dolores had given a donation to the band's funds as a thank-you. So as the auctioneer held up each item it was bid-for by the giver. It was only when the main men of the night were propping up the bar and chatting their way down their second pints that they began to realise that something odd was happening.

Stirling remembered that he had been going to ask Dolores when she bought that bloody frock. He made his way over to her and saw the heap of parcels on her table.

'Now don't you dare ask where all these have come from,' said Dolores crossly. Her cheeks were pink with mixed happiness and annoyance. 'You should notice a bit more what's going on instead of how many pints you can drink. Here. Sit down and look at this.'

She handed him the top parcel from the pile.

Stirling opened it, and his mouth fell open.

'Look. There's a card 'ere 'at says it's for me. By bloody 'ell,' he gasped. 'Hey, look at this. A Kings of Brass tie. Too bloody good for the likes of me. 'Ow come Tommy got hisself a Kings of Brass tie? An' then when he'd getten it, 'e give it to me! By 'eck. I can't get over it.'

'Well you'd better, because you've got a rare pile of other things here. Open this.' She held out an A4 envelope.

'Nay. Somebody's gone an' given me their programme for that National we played in. Wi' signatures from all on us players an' all. Look 'ere, lass.' Stirling sat down heavily on a chair beside his wife.

The programme which was played after the interval was by way of being the band's tribute to their solo horn and flugel players. They started with *Old Comrades*. The familiar opening: Rumph, bum bum

bum bum bumph was thin on sound from the middle of the band. Both Stirling and Horny were struggling.

Bernard introduced the next piece as a nostalgic record, compiled and arranged by Widget for Horny. A few notes from *I've Played the Wild Rover* were followed by snatches from *Sweet Caroline, Mary, Laura, Rosemarie, Daisy, Nancy* and *Dinah*, and culminated in Horny's own splendid and lengthy adaptation of *Annie's Song. Lily of Laguna* was noticeably absent.

'For Stirling,' said Bernard, 'we wanted to put together a few pieces which would show our appreciation of what a great asset he has been to Harden Moss and to the band. So we've chosen a selection of some of the pieces which we have made our own. *Punchinello, Death or Glory*, which we've played at countless Whit Fridays, *Bells Across The Meadow, The Ash Grove*, the solo which Stirling has so often played for us and which Dolores has told me he played at the concert when they first got acquainted, and our favourite hymn tune *Abide With Me*. None of these would ever have sounded right to the followers of Harden Moss Band without the clear notes of our flugel player at their heart.

'We will finish our short tribute concert with *John Miles Music*. Remember the words. 'Music is my first love. It will be my last.' Stirling, this is for you.'

Bernard turned to his bandsmen with his old arms raised in familiar, youthful enthusiasm.

The notes rang sweetly, but a stranger walking up the steep, grey, narrow little lane outside the bandroom might still have wondered at the length and warmth of the cheering which followed as the last sounds died away.